PRAISE FOR COPPING FREE

"Tightly written, fantastic . . . stylized and colorfully scary. . . . If you like Quentin Tarantino films, Hunter Thompson's musings and visits to the Big Top, you'll love *Copping Free*."
—*USA Today*

"[*Copping Free*] speaks for itself, and very little a reviewer can say about it comes anywhere near to matching its hilarious power and flat-out originality. . . . The black fun never flags."
—*Chicago Tribune*

"Authentically badass and yet utterly winning, Matthew Carnahan's *Copping Free* is a ripsnorting neo-noir."
—*Entertainment Weekly*

"Carnahan's got a gift for plot twists. . . . *Copping Free* hits the spot."
—*People* (****)

"[Carnahan has a] talent for odd yet poignant juxtapositions, and throughout the novel, he renders both his characters and the geography of the American West in vibrant high style."
—*Publishers Weekly* (starred review)

"First-novelist Carnahan is a stylist who upgrades pulp to the Turkish-coffee richness of Cain, Hammett, and Chandler."
—*Kirkus Reviews* (starred review)

COPPING FREE

MATTHEW CARNAHAN

A NOVEL

Copping Free

ORIGINALLY PUBLISHED
AS SERPENT GIRL

VILLARD • NEW YORK

2006 Villard Books Trade Paperback Edition

Copyright © 2005 by Matthew Carnahan

Published in the United States by Villard Books,
an imprint of The Random House Publishing Group,
a division of Random House, Inc., New York.

VILLARD and "V" CIRCLED Design are registered
trademarks of Random House, Inc.

Originally published in hardcover in the United States by Villard
Books, an imprint of The Random House Publishing Group,
a division of Random House, Inc., in 2005 under the title
Serpent Girl.

LIBRARY OF CONGRESS CATALOGING-IN-PUBLICATION DATA
Carnahan, Matthew.
    Copping free: a novel / by Matthew Carnahan.
        p. cm.
    ISBN 0-8129-7284-8
        1. Young men—Fiction.   2. Venice (Los Angeles,
Calif.)—Fiction.   3. Swindlers and swindling—Fiction.
4. Circus performers—Fiction.   5. College dropouts—
Fiction.   6. Narcotic addicts—Fiction.   7. Boise (Idaho)—
Fiction.   8. Freak shows—Fiction.   9. Circus—Fiction.
I. Title.
PS3603.A757S49 2005
813'.6—dc22   2004057182

Printed in the United States of America

www.villard.com

9 8 7 6 5 4 3 2 1

OOK DESIGN BY JUDITH STAGNITTO ABBATE/ABBATE DESIGN

FOR HELEN, BECAUSE EVERYTHING IS.

ACKNOWLEDGMENTS

AS IT TURNS out, this book was not written in a cave in secret. I got help, advice, and encouragement along the way from my posse on both coasts. Laurie Lieser took my notebooks full of ravings and tried her very best to decipher them. But best of all, she wanted to know what happened next. The good people at the Twentynine Palms Inn let me write in their restaurant for weeks through their very busy dinner hour. As I worked on the book, I was constantly inspired by my young son, Emmett, and his own dazzling artistic process. My dear friend, the great painter Elliott Green, read the first draft of the manuscript and promptly handed it to a book agent (a group of people I knew exactly zero of) named David McCormick, who was tickled enough to represent it. Dan Menaker and my fellow West Side homie Danielle Durkin edited and guided the book through the publishing process with a sensitivity and sense of play that were astounding to this writer used to the Hollywood hatcheting process. My friends and fellow wave riders Mike Myers, Moon Blauner, Brad Miskell, and Gordon Hunt (and his hot wife, B. J. Ward) were unabashed in their kindness and guidance. And of course, my love, Helen Hunt, has done nothing but gobble up the new chapters and give praise, inspiration, and brilliant feedback throughout.

COPPING FREE

ONE

BLUNT-FORCE TRAUMA

WHEN I CAME to I was squatting and clutching my balls like they were a dangerous little animal that might escape. I was in a burned field under a swirling purple sky, about thirty feet away I could see what appeared to be my pants, methodically folded and waiting for me to come to my senses. I knew at some point I had been in Boise, where I left the circus for good.

I eased my grip and the whole universe started to throb in pain. I grabbed my nuts again and the pain eased. At least that explained that.

Something was wrong with my mouth. My jaw clicked when I tried to move it, and I had the definite tight feeling of dried blood on my neck and chin. I swallowed and my Adam's apple bobbed in a fucked-up, akimbo way. When I made the move to stand, I toppled over onto the scorched earth. The whole lower half of my body was asleep. I lay on the ground looking up at the unreal sky, the UV frying me like a breakfast sausage.

I knew Timbo and Raol had been involved somehow, and not in a good way. When I thought of them my stomach flipped and my squint into the glare became more pronounced, like I was expecting someone to rain down some serious shit from above. And Shane. That insurance-scamming prick. If I had a beer or even a can of iced tea, I could sort this whole thing out. I closed my eyes and when I opened them the sun had sagged in the sky. I could feel a wicked sunburn on the head of my dick—it was screaming obscenities at me in a tiny rage-filled voice. I saw specks moving across the sun. Shading my eyes, I could see they were buzzards, and I dimly realized that dying in the middle of some godforsaken desert was not necessarily just a cliché.

It seemed important to get to my pants, at least as a realistic first goal. I rolled to my side, onto my knees and up to standing. When I got up there I could see more of the world and was bolstered: I was a human being who walked upright, had an opposable thumb, had certain unalienable rights. I had at least three broken toes.

When I got to my pants they seemed to be a ticket back to the rational world. If I could put them on correctly, I would be indistinguishable from other citizens, could even walk among them. They went on smoothly; even the button fly was a breeze.

A semi came hurtling through the middle of the landscape, heat shimmering off its sides. I was near the highway.

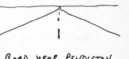

ROAD NEAR PENDLETON

THE HIGHWAY. I had a flicker of memory. Just down the highway was Pendleton. I knew that in Pendleton there was an Indian rodeo cowboy named Tank Deerflower who owed me two hundred bucks. Other than that, there was just blank blackness; my throat, my exit from the circus, my nakedness—nothing brought forth even a dim ray of memory.

I would begin my new amnesiac life by collecting on my debt. The only reason I had any faith Deerflower might pay up was that he was not only a winning rider, he also had a thriving dope business along the Boise–Portland corridor. The only time I had ever dealt with him, he sat in his boxer shorts, treating various rodeo-riding ailments, his feet soaking, arm in a sling, a Glock nine resting on his right thigh. I was buying a quarter pound of his delightful skunkweed, which he described as "monster skull-fuck poop." He treated me like a real client, even though I was small potatoes compared to the amount of boom he moved on a regular basis. But he had shorted me for two hundred bucks' worth. He was known to be a straight dealer, so I had called him, and he had told me straight up that the next time I was in Pendleton, he would square our deal.

He did drift toward the paranoid, though. I started to get chummy and asked where he got such quality stuff in this wasteland.

"These guys are freaky Nam-vet hippie psycho

motherfuckers, and just by asking that question, you have endangered both of our lives and the lives of our families." For emphasis, he made a bug-eyed motion, silently demanding that I say nothing more.

•

I STAGGERED TOWARD the highway and was delighted to find my backpack lying there like an overturned bug, needing me. I dove on the pack, surprising myself with my agility, looking for anything drinkable. There was nothing, just my stinking clothes smelling of elephant shit and sweat, my battered harmonica—an obvious affectation that I flung off into the scrub—and an empty Ziploc with some peyote crumbs. It appeared I had even eaten the little clumps of arsenic on the buttons. I was tripping out of my head.

When I got to the highway, the only vehicle in recent memory was the truck that had boomed through earlier. The ground moved beneath me in disturbing undulations, forcing me to stop and hunker every few yards. I set my pack down and prepared to wait out the day, then the night, and hope for some morning traffic, but an old Malibu snuck right up on me, and before I even stuck my thumb out, it had yanked to a stop a few feet in front of me. I scanned the back for any crazy bumper stickers and humped my pack up to the passenger side. I was conscious of putting on a smile that said Grad Student or something safe, but with whatever had happened to my face, with the peyote skating through my being, I just felt cockeyed and gravidly insane.

The window was opened a crack and a voice boomed out. "Where you headed? Oh, Christ almighty, look at you."

"Vengunntnnnn . . ."

I hadn't spoken in a while, and realized my jaw was definitely dislocated or something.

"Phendledhton . . ." Followed again by the crazy smile.

"Oh, Pendleton. I'm goin' all the way to Portland, get in."

Something in his voice held a desperation that I recognized and feared. When I hesitated, he rolled down the window all the way and said, "It's okay, I'm a police officer. Off duty." He showed me his badge and police

ID. I numbly climbed in the Malibu, hoping I didn't reek of drugs and crime. If I could maintain, I'd have a police escort all the way to Pendleton. Maybe he'd even help me take my cash off Deerflower, take me to Portland, and I could go Greyhound and ride in style up to Seattle and figure this whole mess out.

I glanced at him. He was looking me over, probably running my image against the mug shots pasted up in his office. As far as I knew I wasn't wanted for anything, my problem was the opposite. I had participated in a number of crimes that fill the days of small-town cops but don't really interest them. With Raol and Timbo, we mostly ripped off motorcycles and motorcycle gear from shops. I called it "copping free" because no one got hurt and the big corporate insurance companies paid the tab. The lack of security in most of the places we took off was almost disappointing. Timbo's dad had been a celebrity track biker, and Timbo had spent his early childhood scoping these places out before his dad got in trouble with the IRS and disappeared into South America. Other times we'd buzz around with a glass cutter and grab stuff out of display windows. Copping free. But finally it got so that I couldn't walk down the street without seeing some poor dweeb whose store I had robbed, and the whole thing felt like it was beginning to close in on me.

One day, looking through the help-wanted section in the paper, which I would do from time to time to make myself feel better about copping free, I came across an ad for the circus. In just a few words, it evoked a life on the road, free from crime, college, family, all the moorings that held me in my steady fog of chronic ennui.

So I joined that shithole circus. The circus. A small tide of nausea washed over me, but nothing specific came up.

The Cop was scoping me. I scoured my fried brain for something he could nail me on. The peyote thing might have interested him, but it appeared I had eaten all of it, so I was clean for the moment.

The Cop was either looking at me with pity, or I smelled bad and he was clenching his lower lip to keep from gagging. "What the hell happened to you? Looks like someone had a go at slitting your throat."

I got the feeling he really didn't care, but it was a fair thing to ask an injured hitchhiker.

"Got in a scrap with some buddies." I decided to stick to the whole Grad Student thing. Try to make it sound devil-may-care. My voice was warming up, I could feel the dried blood cracking over my chin, allowing more freedom of movement.

"Buddies, Jesus. I'm Dale. Dale Kuntz." I could tell he had been kidded about the name, because he pronounced it extra hard, like Ra*coons*. His face pulsed in and out from the very center, making his nose go from small to huge, small to huge.

"Sure you're okay?"

"I think I got food poisoning . . ."

"Was that before or after your scrap with your buddies? It's cool, dude, I'm off duty."

Somehow when Dale said "dude," it came up with huge quotation marks around it. I watched them bounce off the low, moldy interior of the Malibu. I laughed and opened the window to let them escape. Now they were free. It was the first and only bit of enjoyment I could remember on this hideous drug trip.

"Manley's Café, y'know, in Boise? I think it was the biscuits and gravy." I hadn't been to Manley's Café since I went with my father one morning right after we moved to Boise.

"If you're gonna get sick, let me know so you don't foul up the 'Bu, awright, dude?"

Again, the quotation marks were plump and frisky.

This time I let them bounce around the car for a while, until they started to oppress me.

"Stop it! Fuckers!" I took a swat at one, causing, I think, real concern on Dale's part.

"Dude—"

"Please don't say that."

"You gotta maintain or get outta my ride, dude . . ."

I realized he must have been toying with me, because the quotation marks were everywhere, small demonic bats diving at my head, and Dale was King Demon, Pitchfork Holder, administering my punishment for eternity.

"Aw, fuck . . . FUCK! Demons!"

"Okay, just lean your head back and close your eyes. And breathe regular." He reached down and opened a cooler by his feet, a mini-Playmate, and pulled out a beer. The sound of the cap sitzing off was like the exhalation of God. Dale handed me the beer and I poured it down my throat. It flowed in so quickly that I felt like a man shot full of holes, impossible to plug.

"It's totally chill, I'm not really a cop. But that badge gets me more pussy than Frank Sinatra."

"He's dead."

"Yeah, but I bet the motherfucker's still gettin' pussy."

Dale cracked two more beers, and we rode and drank in silence for a while.

"Goin' to the rodeo?"

"I guess so . . . yeah . . . rodeo . . ."

I bobbed along nicely, floating on the momentary elation of two beers and a brief leveling of peyote activity. I had to fill in the huge blank space currently occupied by the peyote. Was this an actual blackout? It seemed like I should at least remember someone trying to slash my throat. I tried to drift and let the blackness turn to gray, but got only the shadiest of images: a fast-moving car, a furious elephant rearing and stomping, a Zippo lighter.

I had worked myself into an alpha state when Dale floored the Malibu, and I woke up to an unhealthy grind coming from the bowels of the car. I opened my eyes in time to see Dale coaxing a clip into a .45, its butt crudely duct-taped together.

"Check this shit out."

He was speeding to catch a VW bus, pale yellow and plastered with bumper stickers that showed an appalling optimism.

"Whoa . . . Dale, what's that about?"

"Little college hippie fuckers always have something to share."

"Okay."

I felt the hot puke at the back of my throat before I had time to react. The pathetic gray liquid splashed off the cracked dash and down on the worn floormats.

"Ahhh! Ah, Christ, the Malibu! Dude!"

I had never eaten peyote without yakking, and I felt relieved that I was now exhibiting regular symptoms. Also, the barf seemed to have purged my flying-quotation-mark syndrome along with it, Dale's last "dude" landing in a quiet heap in his lap.

We were right up on the VW bus, and Dale hit a jury-rigged button on his horn that made a siren-squawk noise. The driver of the bus pulled over to the side of the highway without applying the QUESTION AUTHORITY demanded by one of his bumper stickers.

Dale pulled over in front of them and wiggled the gun vaguely at me. I raised my hands limply.

"Stay here an' call in their plates," he said, grinning crazily.

I realized he was playing cop; he was just as whacked as I was, but far more dangerous. He took out his police ID and strode from the car, holding the badge in its cheap wallet, the gun drawn indistinctly, doing his best T. J. Hooker.

"Okay, people, life is short, so let's cooperate, and don't even think about messing with the Law."

There were three girls and two guys in the bus that I could see, and they looked uniformly embarrassed by Dale's opening line. They were hippies with money, that was pretty clear from their freshly shampooed Deadhead look.

Dale was lustily checking out one of the girls, short and pug-nosed, cute, with an impossibly big rack. He leaned over and said something to her; I couldn't hear him, didn't need to. She smiled uncertainly, as if the hidden cameras might emerge at any second. One of the guys, not the driver but a sleepy and stoned-looking passenger, puffed out his chest in a halfhearted proprietary gesture.

"Hey, you gonna give us a ticket or what?" the guy

asked, just a little bit edgy, then he grinned reflexively, looked paranoid, wiped his sleeve across his nose.

Dale responded by pushing past to reach in the van and remove a blue plastic bong. He hooted and held up the bong for me to see, like an Indian scalp or a just-caught trout.

"Whooo! Lookee lookee!" Dale rooted for another few seconds and fished out a decent-sized bag of weed. "Looks like a minimum of two years inside, kiddees!"

Another girl, tall and confident, wearing long Jan Brady braids, was unimpressed by Dale's assessment. "You can't just pull us over and search the van . . . that's like illegal search and seizure."

Dale nonchalantly fired the .45 into one of the headlights of the van. Instead of reacting in horror, the kids, blunted by MTV and Vin Diesel movies, looked on like audience members. Dale started strutting back and forth as if someone were jabbing a stick into his back. He looked like a demented rooster.

I slid over into the driver's seat, held the wheel for a second, looked at the keys dangling in the ignition. I cranked the Malibu, and as I feared, it didn't turn over on the first go.

Dale whipped his head over at me, squinting, like he

couldn't quite believe his ears. "Partner!" he shouted happily, raising the gun and trying to level it off at my head. He started walking casually toward me, licking his lips.

The Malibu turned over on the third try: the mixture way too rich, the sound of the old muscle car parodying itself. Dale turned to the rich hippie kids and smiled, like this was an old joke between partners. He fired a shot at me that sank solidly into the rear quarter panel as I punched the accelerator and watched the small tableau fade to diorama size in the rearview. I saw Dale fire another round, his wrist loose and the gun pointed vaguely skyward.

I ran the car just off the road and struggled for a moment to get off the rough shoulder, swerving back into the lanes and clenching both hands on the wheel. I reached down into the Playmate for another beer. When I had a minute, I would figure this all out, try to piece together what had happened. But for right now I had to get to Pendleton, get my cash, and disappear.

COPPING FREE

TWO

PENDLETON

PENDLETON CAME UP on the right, a sunken-down town set mostly along a draw, some motels and a big ugly mill waiting right off the exit. Most of the year it was a must-miss, featuring the wool mill, bad restaurants, mean bars, and a couple of skanky whores. But during the rodeo, it was a great place to escape the tedium of the area.

Things were happening to my head. My teeth felt like they had grown small and sharp, and I ran my tongue over them obsessively, sucking and wincing. The peyote crash was evil, pure bad, no relief, a relentless physical assault as my various body parts checked in with me to register their complaints. The Malibu was shaking my bones loose from my muscles; Dale had taken such bad care of the car that he deserved to have it stolen. The timing was for shit; the interior, once white, had been buffed to an unsettling taupe by sweat and dirt and spilled Taco Bell.

My puke was warming against the floor, and if I'd had anything left to throw up, I would have let loose. As it was, I was just shy of hanging on, heading toward my two hundred dollars, wondering what the fuck had gone down, how I had left the circus, what violence had been done to me and possibly others.

I was unsure whether I wanted a full recovery of my memory. A tsunami of nausea and dread was sweeping over me. Whatever had happened, my conscious and unconscious mind were locked in a struggle, one to remember, the other to call it blunt-force trauma and leave it at that.

•

I ROLLED CAUTIOUSLY into Pendleton, the Malibu announcing my arrival with a throaty basso profundo bap-bap-bap. It had been a while since I had seen the town, but it really didn't matter. Other than a new Radisson, Pendleton was ossified exactly as it had been the last time I was here.

The place was mobbed for the rodeo. Throngs of tourists in Western wear elbowed uncomfortably, looking for a trinket to buy. But Pendletonians are too stupid to put anything up for sale during the rodeo, other than the same old overpriced wool blankets.

I wanted to dump the Malibu before Dale tracked me, but I also knew that walking more than about a hundred feet was out of the question. Easing off the main drag, I took the poor man's road, moving through a ghetto of Mexican and Indian neighborhoods.

By the time I found Tank Deerflower's place, my head was expanding and contracting like a *Star Trek* alien's. I stepped out of the car and immediately fell to my knees and then comically forward, facedown on the gravel drive.

WHEN I OPENED my eyes, I was entirely sober and I remembered everything. I remembered the gig. I remembered how it had all gone pear-shaped. I remembered that smug abortion of a guy named Shane who got my crew to turn against me.

Tank Deerflower was bitch-slapping me and laughing. Standing over me, he looked like some pagan god carved in burnished copper, shirtless and pantless, wearing only a kind of rodeo-rider girdle, to keep his guts in place, and a dance belt.

"Hey! Looooozzzer!" He was high and broke into a fit of giggles. He slapped me again, not realizing I was wide awake, and I pushed him off. "What the fuck happened to you?"

"I need to learn how to choose my associates more carefully."

"I heard that! I drew a pig-ass bitch of a horse this morning I never should have associated with."

"Right. Kinda like that."

"But let me tell you, bro', that ball-dragging chestnut got me into the semis, second seed."

"That's great . . . Can I hit you up for that two hundred from last time?"

"Your time expired on that shit. That's ancient history."

I think he saw me sinking deep and revised his take on the situation.

"I'll give you a hunny, bro, that's all I can spot you till I kick some neo-Nazi cowboy ass in the finals. You wanna stick around? We got a shitload of hookers coming in from Portland tonight."

"Gonna have to pass."

"That's cool. I bet those ho's wouldn't even go down on you, the way you're looking right now."

"Probably not."

He produced a crumpled hundred-dollar bill and handed it to me. He squinted, looking out the window. "You got hippie friends, Bailey?"

"A couple, I guess."

"Well, they're here."

I heard the sputter of the VW bus and a door slam. "Oh, shit . . . he's got a gun and he's crazy as fuck-all." I scrambled for a spot behind the couch.

Deerflower reached under the sofa cushion and pulled out a matte-black nine-millimeter, fancy, and a sure-to-misfire .22 peashooter, the kind they're always taking away from crackhead boyfriends on *Cops*.

Dale started bellowing from outside the door. "Police officer! You're harboring a dangerous felon, and we will use force to apprehend him!"

Deerflower looked at me, rolled his eyes, and grinned, standing on one side of the door. I stood on the other side and made a cuckoo motion with my finger.

Deerflower put on a cooperative-sounding voice. "Just a minute, Officer, we have the suspect in custody."

Tank stepped over to the open window, and before I could stop him, he fired a single shot in the direction of the front door.

"Aaarraah! Ah, Jesus! Fuck! Fuck! Fuck me! Fuck fuck fuck, shot my fucking foot, fuck fuck fuck fuck!"

"Keys are in it, Dale," I said, relieved.

Dale dragged his bleeding foot across the drive, got in the Malibu, and drove off without another word.

Deerflower looked at me with new respect. "You ain't nobody till you got enemies, Bailey."

"Then I'm definitely somebody."

"That's utterly cool, bro. But you better get the fuck outta here before any more wackos show up looking for you. I gotta get back to the roundup, anyway."

I washed up in Deerflower's kitchen sink as he got his riding gear back on. "Sometimes I feel like I'm too fucking strong." He looked at himself in the mirror.

"Like I could snap the horse in two with my legs, like I could fuck him up just by *telling* him what a badass I am. Keep the peace, bro."

That caught me off guard. "Oh, yeah, peace to you, too, man."

"No, bro, the *piece*. The .22. Sounds like you might need it."

He tossed me a box of shells.

THREE

THE SERPENT GIRL

I SAT IN the VW bus. The blue bong was still there, and I could see Dale had dipped into the weed. I took a roundabout route out of town and headed back toward Idaho. I caught a glimpse of myself in the rearview, turned it toward me, and had a moment of horrible realization. I was twenty-two years old, a college dropout with a partially slit throat. The thing I had most recently feared and wanted—the memory of recent events—was on me. Sometimes you hear people say that memory comes flooding back. But they don't tell you about the other feeling, the feeling of piling up sandbags against the flood, of pointlessly retreating from the tidal wave of memory like some doomed villager. It was all I could do to duck and cover as the memory truck backed up and dumped its load on me.

The guys who were supposed to be my crew, my pals, my posse, had left me for dead after I had gone above and beyond for them, after I had sussed out the perfect score, after I had done my homework, after I had overcome their stupidity, after I had sacrificed my near-virginity by having sex with the Limbless Lady.

Eelie, the Limbless Lady. The piece-of-shit circus I had been traveling with was the last big-top tent circus to tour the country, and one of the last to have a freak show. It had become illegal in certain states, so the Freaks had a lot of time off.

They hung around outside Hamburger Mary's drinking coffee, smoking, eating speed, PCP, and Quaalude, and sexing each other up. This cocktail of drugs was the holy trinity of the circus: The tent crew manufactured their own crystal meth (using something ominously called the Nazi cold-cook method); the PCP was used to tranq the elephants; and the Quaalude they used on the big cats. So these were the commonplace, everyday drugs that kept the circus slam-dancing from town to town.

Hamburger Mary was a vile old cow, three hundred pounds of venomous blubber. She traveled with us and was often the only game in town for meals when the big top was parked out in some abandoned parking lot in East Bumfuck, which was most of the time. She'd charge us above the going rate, then dock it straight off our checks. She had a sweet con going with the circus management.

The Freaks pretty much stuck together and didn't go outside their group for sport. They fought and fucked and every once in a while one of them would shoot another one. They hardly ever died and the police never came. These people were hardwired to be nasty; they completely contradicted the notion that you shouldn't judge a book by its cover. But if they had all been six-foot supermodels, they still would have been freaks. This was the nastiest, most tweaked-out group of mean motherfuckers I had ever come across.

Since they couldn't work in certain states, the Freaks hung out and took an interest in the management of the show. When the owner, a stupid old cokehead named Wayne Stubbs, got in deep financial shit, they pooled their resources and bought him out. They cracked down and immediately started to make money.

Most people come to the circus, sit on the bleachers, eat their peanuts, and space out until someone walks a tightrope or fucks around with a tiger. They don't think about showers or toilets or what the guy in the coveralls does at night after they're safely back home, watching some car chase on the ten o'clock news.

The Freaks eliminated an entire honeywagon—the nice name for the crap trailers—and a whole shower truck. Meaning that suddenly, the crew had to fight, literally, for a place to take a crap. The Freaks were unpopular, but they were used to that, and they were turning a profit.

So, yeah, I boned the Limbless Lady. But that sounds a lot more disgusting than it actually was. I mean, my aim was less than true, and I felt lousy about it, but she wasn't bad-looking. She had a great rack, and looking back, I've often wondered whether her breasts looked so magnificent because there were so few other protrusions to compete with them or if they were great in their own right. Eelie was okay-looking in the face. When she wasn't doing her act and writhing around like a crazed serpent, she took pretty good care of herself.

Eelie, the Limbless Lady, or as her longer professional moniker proclaimed, "Serpent Girl! . . . Eelie, the Limbless Lady! She glides, she writhes, she crawls on her belly like a human snake!" Eelie's act was a big draw. Her husband, Arnold, went by Captain Flame and had a sparsely attended fire act.

Arnold needed Eelie. You'd think she would be the one who needed him, not having limbs and all. But she was, among other things, a wicked online stock trader. She'd find out about a stock and get online, and you'd see her head bobbing up and down on the keyboard, using her tongue and her nose to make the trade. Arnold would just sit there, impressed but resentful, as she made the deal.

FIRE BREATHER

He'd carry her around, cradling her in his arms like a baby. Occasionally he'd get romantic and lean down and they'd tongue the shit out of each other. It was something to see.

LIKE I SAID, I went to bat for my friends. We were punks, friends from Boise High School reunited by our common failure. I was nursing my wounds after getting tossed out of college. Timbo, a good skier and a promising engineering student, had flunked out of Washington State. Raol had never left Boise, choosing instead to drink and drug and wreck himself through an astonishing seven of his parents' cars. And Shane was river-rafting and coasting through the off-season by scamming a series of young women out of places to stay, credit-card numbers, and high-school-graduation Ford Explorers.

We'd sell our copping-free loot in and out of town through a pathetic network of so-called fences—really a bunch of losers who knew the stuff was hot and screwed us on the prices for that very reason.

When I had a bad feeling after one of our rip-offs, I joined the circus to travel a little and let time do its work, figuring I could disappear for a while. It would be my vision quest, roaming the West with a band of merry performers. I would leave behind my criminal ways, settle into a better head, and prepare to start my college career anew. I had been accepted into Boston University as a junior, with some serious reservations on the part of the admissions department, and with a minimum of financial aid. I had absolutely no idea how the fuck I was going to pay for round two of college. I had no savings and no parental help. The circus experience would be my cleansing breath before I returned to academia. I would arrive in Boston on virtual horseback, in a swirl of exotic incense from the beautiful and tarnished circus world, a sociologist, a gypsy. Doe-eyed co-eds would gather in my dorm room to hear me modestly waxing philosophical about the romance of the open road, the "carnie life" (I could just imagine miming big quotation marks with both hands), and my earnest love of "real people." Some rich girl would want to buy me beers and philosophy books.

As it turned out, the circus was a quagmire of desperation, a smoking mobile hell rolling through the baked and polluted landscapes of the West. After maintaining my aloof-observer hoax for a few days, I could no longer hold on to any illusion that I was anything other than a part of it, a willing participant in the destruction of my own dwindling youth.

As I looked around at the way the circus ran, I couldn't help but notice that when the Freaks took over, there was money flowing through the place. Lots of money.

I became obsessed with discovering their methods. After they made their necessary belt-tightening adjustments, the overhead for the show had to be low; then they switched the payroll from checks to cash—probably to do some tax scamming. When I took a look at the whole picture, it occurred to me that I could have my financial aid after all. I pictured my time at Boston University. Instead of working three jobs and setting myself up for failure and nervous collapse, I'd have time to study and money for a phat sound system. Maybe I would have a shot.

Rather than cashing out after every performance, the Freaks would save up for Tuesday, Wednesday, and Thursday. Then they'd take payroll out of that and bank the balance.

As much as I tried, I couldn't figure out where the money went after the shows, and how it made its way to payroll on Fridays. The Freaks were sneaky tight-asses, and they had a scrooge gig working on that cash that I couldn't grasp from my outside spot on props and rigging. I wanted that bank, and I knew the only way in was to get tight with the Freaks. But how would I break into their world? Befriend one? Screw one? I quickly went through the freak roster. There was Eddy, the thin man, a total dweeb who was shunned even by the Freaks. There were the Russian sisters, the Suprova twins, contortionists who considered themselves above freak stature because they had actual skills, and besides, every guy on the crew was hot for them, because who didn't want to bang two chicks who could plant their feet firmly on their own buttocks? There was Bezio, the "world's most tattooed man," who scared the hell out of me. Not only was Bezio mean, like all the other Freaks, but he was smart: book-smart, world-smart, how-to-torture-animals-smart. The guy was well rounded in terms of evil. Among the crowning glories of his all-over tattoos was a pair of rotting, gnarled hands reaching around his neck as if to strangle him. It was like one of his pals from hell was coming to take him back below.

There was Arnold, Eelie's husband, the aforementioned fire guy, who would sooner roast me than befriend me; there was Zoopy, the fattest woman in the world, couldn't hit that; and there was Eelie, the Limbless Lady. Bingo. It sounded as clearly as the bell in a Buddhist temple. I could just feel her need and her loneliness, and really, she was kind of hot in her own way.

Eelie was not, in actuality, limbless. She had a couple of workable flipper-type jobs for arms, one of them even sporting a near-opposable thumb. For legs she was less fortunate: They were simple round stubs, smooth as baby ass.

FOUR

XANA CALIPATRIA

WHEN I ROLLED the VW bus into Mountain Home, I felt like I was wearing a hatchet in the center of my forehead. I had stopped at Denny's for a Grand Slam, which was sitting so-so in my stomach. I had occupied the bathroom there for half an hour and tried to get myself to a slightly more presentable state. I washed my neck until all that remained was a ragged line where my boys had screwed up my murder. The wound was relatively superficial, but I'd have to keep it clean. There wasn't much to do about the broken toes other than favor them.

I looked into my own eyes, red and somehow imprinted with new information, a kind of brand seared into the center of me. But this information, unlike most, only served to bring me further from myself.

I sat at the plastic booth at Denny's, praying that no passing highway patrol would catch a look at the VW bus, which I had parked, plates in, all the way behind the Dumpsters. I was so paranoid about the cops and the hippie kids looking for their ride that I couldn't really enjoy my first meal back among the living.

Mountain Home is neither homey nor in the mountains. It's a grubby town full of survivalists and lumber workers and a third-rate military base. I was looking for Xana Calipatria, and she fit into none of these categories. Xana was Shane's girlfriend, and I knew I could find either him or where he was by making a stop at her place. Shane would be the key to this thing. Timbo and Raol, though I would not describe either of them as good people, were not criminal masterminds.

I parked the bus a good quarter mile away, pocketed

the .22, and hoofed toward what Shane referred to as the Lust Shack, Xana's tiny house set back from the road in a lot full of weeds. It was familiar to me, but looked wrong in the daylight. I was used to the place at night, as a kind of party central. I moved in quietly and walked around back, looked in the window.

Xana was butt-naked, moving around her place, getting dressed. How Shane wound up with a stellar piece of ass like Xana was one of life's mysteries. She had her bush waxed in the landing strip fashion, not my personal preference, but she wore it well. Some guys liked that, some went for the totally shaved beav—too prepubescent for me—while I personally liked to bungle in the jungle. Not that I had a tremendous amount of experience, but I had spent enough time gazing at magazines and loping the mule to know what got me going.

Xana disappeared from view and then appeared almost directly in front of me, going through her bureau for clothes. She looked in the mirror, and I could see that her breasts were bruised. They reminded me of mangoes when they're ripe and perfectly juicy. She put on a pair of thong panties, and the landing strip disappeared.

After she put on cutoffs, she housed the mangoes in

a Wonderbra and a midriff T-shirt, and she disappeared from view again. The more clothing she put on, the less good-looking she got, but she knew that and kept it to a minimum. I figured she might be going out, so if I wanted to talk to her, it had to be now.

I opened the back door quietly and followed the sounds of water to the kitchen, where she had just finished making coffee.

"Hey, Xana," I said, trying to sound casual.

She jumped and spun around like I'd grabbed her ass. "Bailey! Jesus, you scared me."

"Sorry."

"Want some coffee?"

"Yeah, okay."

She poured the coffee and I watched her carefully. If she knew anything about what had gone down, she was playing it way cool. Without asking, she put in milk and sugar—she was right—and handed me my coffee. It was the real deal, rich and near-Turkish.

"This is good," I said. "I wouldn't have figured you for the domestic type."

She smiled. "I only do a few things well."

"Well, if this is any indication, the other few things must be impressive."

"How long have you been wanting to fuck me?"

I just stared back at her. She didn't want or need an answer.

"Since the first time you saw me?"

I nodded slightly. What was she doing?

She slid her hand down my chest and over the .22 before coming to rest between my legs.

"Ooh. You've got a gun in your pocket *and* you're glad to see me."

She gave me a deadeye sex stare, something I had only ever witnessed at the multiplex, by overpaid actors.

"What're you—"

"So . . . Shane threw me one lousy fuck and left . . ."

My dick and my brain were locked in mortal combat. I knew she was probably helping Shane right at this moment. He was probably outside, or getting away, or behind me with a baseball bat or one of his gangsta gats.

"I should get going," I said.

My dick won. I had completely forgotten why I was here, but her body, her scent, her coffee, were giving me reasons to stick around.

"One for the road?"

"Where'd you get the bruises?" I asked.

She glanced at her arms and legs, which were unbruised, and slapped my arm playfully. "Bailey, you've been peeking."

"A little."

"A little goes a long way."

"You didn't answer my question."

"Shane's an animal."

"Yeah." I could just picture Shane's feathered hair stringy with sweat as he manhandled Xana's tits with one hand and waved his gun with the other.

"But you wouldn't know about that, would you? You're a nice boy."

No matter how rotten I got, people always thought I was a nice boy. I tried different haircuts, wore rude T-shirts, even painted my fingernails black once, but most people still assumed I was an Eagle Scout.

"Let's go," I said.

She got on the bed and waited for me, striking a more lurid version of a Victoria's Secret pose. "Are you just gonna stand there, or are you actually gonna fuck me?"

I climbed on the bed and started kissing her. Her tongue was rigid and hyperactive, and her mouth tasted of cigarettes and that coffee, with a trace of what could have been last night's Jägermeister. But as I said, Xana was all about body. She unhooked her bra and her bruised mangoes spilled out. I pulled off her panties and the landing strip lay before me. I was getting an okay-for-takeoff from the control tower.

THONG

"Aren't you gonna take off your clothes?" Xana asked.

"No," I said, diving on her perfectly trimmed muff.

I got busy going down on her, and she seemed to forget that I was dressed.

•

I LAY ON Xana's bed thinking about my plan and realized I didn't really have one. Xana had dozed off, and in repose she looked sad and vaguely hopeful. Her skin was large-pored and her nostrils almost porcine. I had a rush of what felt like real affection for her.

"I gotta go," I said, nudging her slightly.

"Mmm," she said.

"I need to know where those guys went. Shane and Timbo and Raol."

COPPING FREE

She started to wake up. "Why? I thought you were going to Boston."

"Boston?"

"Yeah. Shane said you took your share and headed to some college in Boston."

This was news to me, but I decided not to let on.

"Oh, yeah," I said. "I decided to defer for a semester."

"So, you gonna catch up with those guys and get in more trouble?"

"Yeah. Maybe."

"You should leave those guys behind. Go back to college."

I couldn't tell if this was a warning, a misdirect, or an actual bit of concern.

"How about I plan my own schedule, Xana?"

"Awright, tough guy."

"So where are they?"

She sighed heavily. "You remember Rick Dellard?"

"No."

"That geeky guy used to be a barback at Desmond and Molly's?"

"Right, yeah."

"Well, now his name is Nik Slave, and he's got this

band called the Manscouts of America down in L.A., some kinda neo-glam hair band."

"You got his number?"

"I guess."

She got out of bed and I watched her move across the house, totally uninhibited and splendid. She came back with a piece of paper and handed it to me.

"Do me a favor and don't tell Shane I stopped by. I want to surprise him."

"Yeah, sure, Bailey, I'm gonna tell him you stopped by and banged the shit outta me."

"I'll see ya around."

She fished around in the sheets for her panties. "Y'know what? That was all right. Shane never eats me out."

"Thanks."

I let myself out while Xana got dressed, and headed for Los Angeles.

FIVE

I Am a Vigilant, Righteous, In-Your-Face Motherfucker

I DROVE AT night and found secluded spots to crash during the day. I figured the pseudo-hippie kids had written down the license plate of the Malibu, and that Dale had been busted by now and maybe the cops and the insurance company were satisfied. I had fallen in love with the bus; it was comfortable, drove honestly, got predictably bad mileage, and came with a wardrobe.

I even found another $190 in a makeup bag. I tossed the weed and the bong. I hadn't even touched a beer after my peyote experience. Those fuckers in L.A. would be dealing with the sober Bailey Quinn, the straight-edge Bailey Quinn, the vigilant, righteous, in-your-face motherfucker who would make them pay. They were holding—assuming they had not whored and snorted it away—in excess of forty-five thousand dollars, half of which, according to our deal, was mine, because I set it up, did the due diligence, and boned the Limbless Lady.

AFTER DECIDING THAT Eelie would be my way in to the Freaks, I set about placing myself in her path as often as

I could during the times she wasn't with Arnold, which were few. She had a skateboard someone had rigged for her to push along with her flippers, and as luck had it, I was a skate-boarder, too. I used a Sector Nine longboard to get around the malls and parking lots that the big top parked in during our gigs. It was one of the few things I allowed myself to keep from our smash-and-grabs. I was pretty proficient on it, and since it was a downhill board, about five feet long, I didn't feel any pressure to jump around doing ollies and assaulting handrails and stairs.

One day as Eelie was scooting herself along from Hamburger Mary's back to her trailer, I managed to skateboard at a perfect perpendicular to her.

"I like your board," I said, smiling my best nice-but-sexy-guy smile.

"Wanna race?" She smiled wryly, squinting up at me.

"You'd probably kick my ass," I said.

"Honey, I don't kick anything," she said, glancing down at her stubs.

"Sorry, I meant—"

"That was a joke there, tiger. Don't worry about it."

I smiled again, thankful for being let off the hook.

"But as penance, why don't you give me a hand getting into my trailer."

I tried to look put upon, just so she didn't see me mentally high-fiving myself. I glanced at my watch. "Um, we gotta run a rigging check . . . Let's see, yeah, I'm cool. No problem."

I watched her face as I went through my bogus calculations. I could tell that she was a woman who was used to a panoply of disappointments. But when I said okay, I saw her light up a little. I had chosen perfectly.

·

THERE'S A RIGID caste system in the circus, and as a crew member, I was one of the untouchables. Performers never associated with crew, with a few exceptions. The performers who depended on my crew, like the tightrope and trapeze artists, learned our names and tipped us on holidays. But if they saw us in a bar, they wouldn't even consider sitting down with us. It would be like some Park Avenue aristocrat partying with the doorman. The only performers who associated with the crew were a few of the showgirls who wore the stupid feathered headdresses and rode around on the elephants during the parade. Three of them were hookers, and in addition to their salaries, they pulled in a healthy sum by servicing those members of the crew who would sacrifice a large percentage of their paycheck to get a mediocre bang.

Performers had their own trailers and motor homes, their own kitchens and bathrooms, and they parked on the other side of the lot from us crew grunts. We were stacked on shelves in the back of large tractor trailers. Your shelf held all your shit, and you, when you were sleeping. My shelf had just enough room for me to turn over. When I read a book, I had to hang it off the side. But I got so much grief that I stopped reading completely.

So even though I was with a Freak, the Limbless Lady, a larva of a woman, she was the one who was associating below her station.

There was a small platform rig for Eelie to get inside the trailer unassisted, but it was apparently a pain to use. When we got to the trailer, she said, "Now, this is where it gets a little awkward. If I could get you to pick me up . . ."

I lifted her up and held her. She was a compact package, and there was something that was a huge turn-on about holding this woman who was, for the moment, entirely dependent on me.

"This is nice," I said, surprising myself and, I think, surprising Eelie.

"Feels okay to me, too," she said.

I carried her inside. Eelie and Arnold's trailer was strange. There were two distinct worlds, one for Arnold, and one at about ankle level for Eelie.

"You can just . . . put me down on the bed, if you don't mind," she said.

The bed was low, with a kind of slide running down from the mattress. It gave the illusion of fun and play, though I imagined the reality was tougher.

I went to deposit Eelie gently in the center of the bed. As I laid her down, I had to put my knee on the mattress; she noted it. "As long as you keep one foot on the floor." I think she also noticed, as I certainly had, that I was sporting some wood.

Eelie smiled and exhaled, resting from her journey. "We haven't ever been formally introduced," she said. "I'm Eelie."

"Bailey Quinn." I didn't know whether to extend a hand, so I froze. Eelie rolled partway onto her side and extended her flipper that had a thumblike appendage.

"It's okay," she said.

I took her flipper-hand and held it in mine. It was as smooth and cool as beach glass.

"It's really nice to meet you," I said.

"Likewise."

"I'm, uh . . . on the crew."

"Props and rigging, right? I was watching you work the bull tubs. Not bad."

Bull tubs are the round metal platforms that the elephants stand on to do tricks. They were my least favorite part of the job, and that was saying a lot, considering how shitty my job was.

"Yeah, I started here the week that guy Kenny got his toes cut off when he rolled one over his foot."

"Ouch," she said unenthusiastically.

After I watched Kenny get hauled away, I took it upon myself to get really good on the bull tubs. They were heavy as hell, so the only way to move them was to roll them, steering with the smaller platform circle. It made me feel like a newborn baby trying to drive a truck. I was amazed that Eelie had ever noticed me, a lowly propman wrestling with crap-covered bull tubs.

"Anyway, I gotta get rigging," I said.

I excused myself, beating a hasty retreat back outside and bombing through the truck corridors on my board. Why the hell would I get a hard-on from helping the Limbless Lady into her creepy trailer? I wrote it off as young-guy-who-hasn't-been-laid-in-a-long-time syndrome, remembering that I had cranked up a chubby while watching the poodle ballet a few weeks earlier.

SIX

THE HAPPIEST PLACE ON EARTH

DESCENDING INTO THE San Fernando Valley on the southbound 101, I was filled with a conflicted sense of sadness, childlike optimism, and rage.

I realized that the childlike optimism and sadness were a flashback to the only other time I had ever been to Los Angeles. I was about nine or ten, and it was the one vacation my family took together. It was as close to happy as I ever got. My mom, an artsy type, got two empty ice-cream tubs from 31 Flavors and filled them with activities and art supplies for me and my brother. My brother's sense of personal vengeance hadn't kicked in yet; he was a preadolescent who beat the crap out of me whenever he got the chance, but he was nowhere near as bad as he would get later. We took the wayback of the old Chevy wagon, two sleeping bags lying side by side, and colored and made stupid tape recordings and played crossword puzzles the whole trip down from Walnut Creek, where we lived at the time.

We were bound for Disneyland, the Happiest Place on Earth, and when I was nine, that was exactly what it was. I was already old enough to think Mickey Mouse was an asshole, but I was also tall enough to hit all the rides and young enough to be scared and amazed by them.

Remarkably, my brother never drew an imaginary border across the car, where if I'd crossed I'd have been treated like an ethnic Albanian. It was almost as if he liked me, a feeling I never experienced before or since.

Because our dad was in industrial relations at the time and had some special connections, for some reason we got to take a helicopter from Burbank out to Anaheim and Disneyland. Even as we took the helicopter ride, my brother and I got along, pretending to be tail-gunners in Desert Storm, kicking ass in an Apache attack chopper. Neither of our parents told us to shut up, and our dad never reached over and gave one of his famously stinging slaps to the side of the head. We stayed at what must have been the official Disneyland hotel. It had paddleboats and ducks and geese, and my brother and I were free to sail paper airplanes out the eleventh-story window with pleas for help or treasure maps written on them.

Our parents must have been boning a lot or something, because they'd let us go downstairs for breakfast by ourselves, with a wad of cash. We would order obscene things like strawberry waffles buried in whipped cream and syrup, and bacon covered with hot fudge.

At the park, we'd spend days and nights hitting all the rides, our parents laughing and watching us from the little faux-intimate cafés as we mugged while they took pictures and video and drank coffee.

Not long after we got back from that vacation, our dad got busted by our mom for doing his "executive assistant," a leathery-faced woman named Pam who winced when she smiled.

The affair pretty much drove a stake through the heart of our family, not that it was perfect before, but it sent my brother into a Charles Bronson–style state of hostility and anger. And our mom, who had spent our whole childhood making sure everything was exactly so—kind of a Martha Stewart pioneer—lost her shit for a while.

I came home after school one day, and I heard a strange animal moaning in the back of the house. It was a sound I had never in my life heard before, a keening-laughing-weeping smorgasbord of extremes.

"Mom?" I asked, hoping somehow it was not her.

She was soaking in the tub, thrashing around in a bouillabaisse of angst, her eyes puffy red and crazy.

"Bailey? Bailey, is that you?" she asked.

"Yeah, Mom, I'm right here."

"No!" She writhed around. "There's nothing out there! Oh God, oh God. I'm dying! I'm dying! Or am I already dead?"

"No, Mom, you're fine. You're in the bathtub."

"Your father is leaving us," she said.

I nodded. "No way," I said, though it sounded like exactly what I'd expected.

"So much blood . . ." she said.

I looked, but there was no blood that I could see. "Mom, you're okay."

"Bailey, don't try to bring me back! I'm dying!"

I backed out of the bathroom. I could call Mrs. Coyle, our neighbor and a pretty good friend of my mom's, but I had no protocol for insanity. Something about it felt private, obscured by a darkness I had until then only suspected. I passed through the kitchen and grabbed a package of graham crackers, wrote something on the memo pad on the counter.

I tried to call my dad at his office in San Francisco, but I got his voice mail. I went up to the pool and fired my wrist rocket at screeching blue jays.

THE ODD THING is, when my dad came home from work the next day, my mom was antiquing the trim in the kitchen, and life proceeded exactly as it had before. My dad didn't leave us. But something was changed in a way that felt as if our lives had been hollowed out like a jack-o'-lantern.

•

AFTER I GOT booted out of college, I visited my parents' house on the way back to Boise to do some copping free. I spent my days smoking dope and watching TV. One day I got high and started looking through my mom's stuff. She had a little wooden box buried under a lot of jewelry. I guess it was the place she had kept anything to do with that time of her life, the time of my dad's affair. There were angry poems, a couple of half-finished letters, some weird drawings, and the memo pad I had written on after she told me. All it said was, written in pencil, I CAN'T BELIEVE IT. Even then I was not the most profound guy in the world. But I guess the reason she hung on to it was that the pencil had dug deep, through about twenty pages of the memo pad. I looked at my childhood scrawl and simply could not remember writing it. I put everything back in that box really carefully.

•

L.A. WAS COVERED with what looked like the dregs of a café latte, a mocha-colored layer of haze that ended abruptly at the heights of the highest buildings, giving way to a less distinguishable and probably far more toxic haze. I had no idea where I was going, except that Xana thought Nik Slave lived in Venice somewhere. I looked at my map and took the 405 over the hills, making my way toward the beach.

I felt like some Special Forces secret operative, parachuting in on the unsuspecting city of Los Angeles. I felt righteous and emboldened in my task; I was now in the unusual (for me) position of being the one who had been wronged. By the time the good citizens of Los Angeles realized what had happened, I would be deep into my studies in Boston, once again living my civilian life, with more of my tuition paid. Raol, Timbo, and Shane were out there somewhere, the three of them, carelessly spending my dough. I thought of Raol's tightly curled hair, his half-Pakistani scowl. He had a seriously bad attitude, and I was going to make it worse. And Timbo—a cross between Shaggy and Scooby—I would smack his pretend guilelessness right off his face. But the majority of my wrath would belong to Shane, the alpha a-hole of the pack. There had to be a special humiliation in store for him. I had already—miraculously—banged his girlfriend. That would be just the beginning.

SEVEN

CHEAP TRICK

I STOOD ON the corner of Rose Avenue and Lincoln Boulevard in Venice, California, with no idea which way to go. This was a part of town I had never encountered on my Disneyland trip. Lincoln was one of those stretches of road that demonstrated the appetites of a big-car-driven town. This was where the monster grazed: gas stations, auto-parts stores, radiator shops, windshield glass, used cars, car rental. In its own sad way, it was entirely self-contained, also providing the greasy dives where the schleps who worked in these places could poison themselves. From what I could scope of the street action, it held all the recreational drugs and low-end hookers the boys could ever need. In fact, one of them was checking me out, clearly thinking I looked like the typical trick-on-a-budget. She sidled up alongside me, pretending to read a flyer that implored, MOVIE EXTRAS NEEDED! She got close. Too close.

I edged toward the phone booth, and she asked, "You're not a cop, are you?"

I looked at her. "Yeah, vice."

She liked that one. "And I'm the first lady."

"The first lady of what?"

"What do you think?"

"Look," I said, "you're not gonna score any cash off me. I'm broke, and I don't have the time."

"Ooh, big diss. I'm mortally wounded. What made you think I was looking to get cash off you, anyway?"

I rolled my eyes, getting out some coins so I could make a phone call. For a minor boulevard hooker, she was okay. Bad dental work and a couple of botched tattoos, but beautiful long red hair and piercing blue wolf eyes. She scared me.

"I'm Sissy," she said. She extended her hand playfully, cocking her hip to one side.

"Bailey." I shook her hand. It was as rough as an itinerant farmworker's, but slender and agile. She was wearing a total hippie-girl getup: nose ring, cotton batik-print shirt, army-surplus cargo pants, and a whole shitload of import-store jewelry. I guessed some johns were into that look.

"Just so you know, I don't want anything from you," she said.

I nodded, looking into those wolf eyes.

"Anyway," I said, suddenly saddened by the thought of this girl hoovering cock on side streets for twenty bucks a pop.

"You're not from around here," she said, not even asking.

"No, I'm not."

"Well, here's my pager number, if you want to get a latte or anything."

"Thanks," I said, surprised by her uncomplicated offer. I watched her saunter off in her trashed Birkenstocks. She could have been any of hundreds of Deadhead girls I went to college with, except for those sand-paper hands and a couple grand in dental. I crumpled her number and jammed it in my pocket, taking out Nik Slave's number, written in Xana Calipatria's postcoital scrawl. The phone rang only about one half-ring before Nik answered, hyper and probably speeding.

"Yeah?" he said.

"Is this . . . Richard Dellard?" I asked, trying to sound businesslike.

"No. This is Nik Slave. It's Nik Slave now."

"Oh, I'm sorry," I said. "This is Johnny Delficcio from Western Cable."

"I don't have cable," he said, getting ready to termi-nate.

"I thought someone had already spoken to you about the free cable."

"Free cable?"

Bingo. I remembered Rick Dellard as a video-game and TV freak.

"Yeah, we're offering free cable for six months if you're willing to fill out a customer-satisfaction report every six weeks." I had no idea what I was saying.

"Fuck," he said, "that's cool."

"Yes, it is."

"Do I hafta wait around all day and you guys show up at, like, midnight?" He was already annoyed.

"No, Nik, you don't. I can slot you in at nine A.M. tomorrow."

"Nine A.M.? That's way early."

"After that I can only give an approximate time from noon to eight P.M."

"Okay, nine is cool."

"And your address again is?" I asked.

"Eighteen Clubhouse Avenue. Three B. What's your name again?"

"Johnny Delficcio. I'll be the one with the tool belt." I laughed a cheezy cable-guy laugh.

"Right," he said.

"See ya then . . . milk, two sugars . . ."

"Huh?"

"My coffee!" I shouted cheerfully.

He hung up and I dropped my happy Johnny Delficcio demeanor. I had a lot to do before morning.

EIGHT

COPPING FREE

I WAS SLEEPING peacefully in a parking lot in Venice, where the traffic sounded almost like the quiet roar of the ocean. Maybe I really was hearing the ocean. Either way, I was nestled in the bus, a pile of laundry for my bed, more space than I'd had in months, when I heard the squawk of a police cruiser. I sat bolt upright, looked out the window, and saw LAPD rousting some bums, making their way toward the bus.

I could fire up the bus and drive away, but I was pretty sure they'd come after me. My other option was to play Mr. Nice Guy and hope they didn't run the plates or haul my ass in. I looked at the pile of laundry. I had one other option.

When the Five-O got to the bus, they shone their flashlights all around. They rapped on the window loudly, one of them calling out in his best cop voice: "Hello . . . sir or ma'am? Can we get you to open up, please? We need you to open up, please. Open the door, please."

I was lying under the pile of laundry, stock-still. I could hear the jangling of utility belts as the cops shifted around impatiently. Their flashlight beams fell on my laundry pile and held there.

"It's just clothes and crap," said one cop.

After I heard them jingle off, I lay there under the rank laundry for a while, thinking I might be able to doze off again. When I realized that wasn't going to happen, I started to wake up and assemble my assault on Nik Slave. It was odd that he would be a player in my revenge story. I could barely remember what he looked like as Rick Dellard, back in the day in Boise. He had been one of those kids in the deep background who only distinguished himself by tripping and falling or by drinking a giant load of bongwater just to get a reaction.

From one of the thrift stores on Lincoln, I had gathered what—at least to Nik Slave, fucked-up wannabe glam-rocker musician at nine A.M.—might pass for a cable-guy outfit. Navy blue 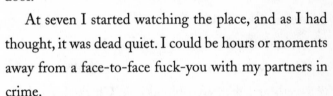 work pants and shirt, a gimme cap, a pair of aviator mirrored shades, a homemade tool belt with some pieces of cable, and a few old tools. All I had to do was get in the door.

At seven I started watching the place, and as I had thought, it was dead quiet. I could be hours or moments away from a face-to-face fuck-you with my partners in crime.

•

I'D HAD THE idea for the rip-off in Chicago, and I worked it all out during the tour, slow and deliberate, amassing all the information toward D-day in Boise. I even made a big show of leaving the circus while it was in Yakima, telling them I was going back to see my family in Seattle and return to college. After I left, I hooked up with my old copping-free buddies in Boise, Timbo and Raol, who insisted that Shane get involved because he had more experience than the three of us. Shane was our age but came from Virginia during our senior year in high school, where he said he had done some time for a big rip-off of sports equipment from a semi-pro stadium. He also claimed to have pulled off a couple of successful armed heists, but they sounded bogus to me. As I laid the plan out for them, I could tell Shane wanted to take over. I didn't let him, not out of any particular ego trip but because I knew it down to how many breaths to take. This one was mine, and he was lucky to be going to the show.

Shane was a wiry little fuck, perpetually tan, with big teeth and feathered blond hair. Chicks loved him. He worked as a guide on Salmon River rafting trips and was always quick to throw in a rafting metaphor whenever he could, whether or not it was appropriate to the situation.

Timbo and Raol seemed unusually enamored of Shane, even though he rarely said or did anything particularly meaningful. He made me nervous; he was always strapped with a flashy chrome nine that he liked to take out and whip around like a spare cock whenever he got the chance, saying something like "This bitch'll get you through the rapids."

Because I didn't worship him for his rafting and gun-toting prowess, Shane fucked with me, trying to undermine me with Timbo and Raol. One time when we broke into an assayer's lab where Raol used to work, to huff some nitrous oxide, Shane started trying to get into the locked mineral samples, looking for gold and silver nuggets. I told him that any precious minerals would be in the safe; why didn't he try to blow it? He was speeding and took out one of his guns and started waving it at me, telling me I didn't know shit about copping free.

In reality, it was Shane who didn't know dick about copping free. Copping free was a way of life. Copping free was my whole thing, my personal ethos, and for Shane to even utter the phrase was an act of war. My whole copping-free philosophy was that you never really took anything from anyone. If you're copping free, you can't take someone's wallet or their life. The circus job was right at the edge of the envelope, because the Freaks were undoubtedly insured, and had skimmed and scammed their way to profit, but other than Eelie, I didn't care much about those bottom dwellers.

I told Shane if he was referring to the fact that I hadn't done hard time for stealing football helmets, he was right. I said I hadn't realized that if you wanted to be a big-time rip-off artist, you had to play French maid for Bubba on the ward. This seemed to strike a painful chord for Shane. He racked one into the chamber and straight-armed the piece at me.

"That right?" he asked, staring me down. "Maybe I oughta make you my bitch right now, huh, Miss Bailey?"

Luckily, at that moment, Timbo had a seizure from huffing too much nitrous, and the moment passed without me taking a bullet. But it was always like that with Shane, and I was a fucking numbskull for ever letting Timbo and Raol talk me into giving Shane a piece of the action. Because I had the circus gig nailed.

The day we hit the circus, it was all good. God or the devil was smiling down on us. We came in like the A-Team, organized and top-heavy with attitude. I had laid down the law with my co-robbers over the past several weeks. Number one, no weapons. We'd rigged up some flares to look like dynamite, and each of us held a taped bundle to threaten the payroll goons with. I made Shane leave his favorite killing accessory at home. As a concession, I let him hold the plastic gun, which looked plenty threatening from the wrong end. If we were busted, we would do minimal time for unarmed robbery. Plus, the whole notion of killing people was as unimaginable to me as it was unappealing.

Number two, establish total and utter chaos. We staged a fake break-in and started a fire on the far side of the compound, so we'd have a smaller crowd for showtime. Three, hit during the show, while all the performers and crew were occupied, and the payroll crew was busy prepping the envelopes.

We went in with clown makeup and rubber gloves, no ID, no prints. All my preparation paid off to the tune of forty-five large and some change.

•

WHEN SHANE BUSTED through the trailer door, followed by the rest of the crew, there was a long moment of quiet, with lots of uncomfortable smiles as people went from thinking it was all a gag to stark pants-pissing terror. I didn't feel good about the terror part; I never got off on scaring people and being the puppet master. But I needed a hit. I needed it *that* bad, so I could clear out of Boise and blow out of town.

When I moved into the trailer, in full clown makeup, wig, and wraparound shades, I was face-to-face with my old buddy Arnold. Shane was playing cowboy pretty well, so nobody was going for weapons. I knew Baby, the security guy, carried a sawed-off, so I motioned for Shane to cover him. Baby was a steroid-addled muscleman, loyal to the Freaks as a blind pit bull. Baby looked at Shane in his getup.

"Hey, Clownie Boy," said Baby, "you scared?"

"Fuck no, you shrunken-dicked muscle fuck."

"You really gonna shoot me, Clownie Boy?"

Of course, Baby had to go pick a fight with the most aggro member of our crew.

Shane was looking apoplectic because he couldn't actually shoot Baby, thanks to the fake gun.

"Just keep your hands right there, big man, and nobody's gonna shoot anybody," I said, trying to sound confident while disguising my voice.

Out of the corner of my eye, I saw Arnold turning slowly to look at me, some flicker of recognition sparking behind his flat eyes. Fuck.

Raol stood stupidly, holding his "dynamite," while Timbo loaded the duffel with money: worn, green, sexy, nonsequential, non-dye-packed money.

The next few moments unfolded like some frame-by-frame Wide World of Sports super slo-mo of the agony of defeat.

Shane started doing bar tricks with his Zippo. Flipping it open and closed, doing a little quick-light deal with it, then waving it near Raol's taped-up package. Baby was getting nervous and pissed off.

"You skinny little cunt, you ain't got the balls," he said. "You ain't even got the balls to pop a cap in me, you sure as hell ain't got the balls to blow this place up."

"I ain't got the balls to put a cap in your ass? That right, you fuckin' Mr. Clean?" Shane reached down to his ankle for another gat, this time a real one, a hardcore snub-nose. He unfurled his arm at Baby, who for the first time gave up his macho mask and looked like he might crap himself.

Timbo and Raol were crabbing out of the trailer, Timbo with the still-unzipped duffel, and Raol behind him with a glazed-over look of panic.

As Shane drew a bead on Baby, I lunged and hit his arm the second the hammer came down. The little gun blew out the fluorescent overhead, raining small, brittle shards of glass down on the payroll geeks. I grabbed Shane's Zippo, which he had dropped to go for his ankle piece.

I lit my bundle of flares, brandished them, and threw them into the trailer as I fled, in time to see the trailer full of bean counters diving for the floor.

NINE

ÇHAGGUS INTERRUPTUS

MY COLLEGE CAREER was cut short at the beginning of my junior year, due to a fiasco that never would have happened if I had listened to my dad and pledged Sigma Chi. It wasn't Sigma Chi in particular, it was the whole Greek thing. I had a violent allergy to it from the moment I stepped onto campus my freshman year. The upperclassmen in the fraternities were smug and vicious, and the young pledges were equally repugnant, following the older guys around like eager catamites. In my first several days of college, I witnessed spankings, dunkings, fires, and a dozen or so public music and dance performances by young drunk guys in drag. My small group of friends from the dorm took a particular dislike to the frat boys, and we began a campaign our freshman year that culminated in my dismissal from the university.

We held a key strategic position between fraternity and sorority rows on the small campus, so we were able to wreak havoc on the bizarre romantic rituals between the houses, which was one of the few activities they approached in earnest. There were strange mating dances involving old songs, formal wear, candlelight vigils, and jockstraps. We were almost always able to disrupt them with vats of Jell-O, water balloons, or earsplitting raunchy Zappa tunes. It was war. We were as divided as the Hutus and Tutsis, along lines that were almost as indecipherable. We were mostly Democrats and Green Party types, with a few genuine anarchist radicals thrown in; they were, for the most part, Republicans. They were hard-drinking kegger and Jägermeister fans; we were drug fiends. We were living on a steady diet of E and mushrooms while they were afloat in a pool of Bacardi.

That was probably the substantive difference, even though we liked to think that they were somehow The Man, trying to keep us down. The truth was, we were all middle-to-upper-middle-class kids looking for something to do after class. We drank a lot, too; it just wasn't the substance that defined us.

My girlfriend at the time, Carin Schlosser, was a ballet dancer and about as cute as any girl I ever got near in college. I was in love, or I was in love with my burning desire to have sex with her. (At that point the two were indistinguishable to me.) I was always bugging her to do it, and in order to shut me up, sometimes she would intimate that someday she might let me. One night we were in her room, a couple of candles burning and some mellow music playing, and I managed to get her completely naked. I was marveling at the beauty of her dancer's body as I went through the motions of giving her a "massage." Finally she rose up on all fours and said, "You can put it in me now," which may in retrospect not be the most romantic words ever uttered, but at that moment they absolutely worked for me. I was entering her from behind when the room flooded with bright light. The hooting and shouting and cheering started immediately. The Sigma Chi boys stood outside on the flat roof holding big halogen work lights. Laughing and fist-bumping and woof-woof-woofing.

I don't remember much after that. But I know I very politely said "Excuse me" to Carin Schlosser, who was by this time covered up and maybe not even all that upset. She was, after all, probably a virgin and had been about to give it up for a guy who, though I hate to admit it, was not exactly the campus stud.

I have memories that come in strobelike images. Flipping every piece of furniture in the Sigma Chi entryway. Taking my Buck knife to some hundred-year-old painting of a patrician-looking fraternity founder. Holding the knife to the neck of a pledge; ironically, the younger brother of a friend of mine from back home. Seeing the tears in his eyes and feeling foolish. I'll never forget his frozen, coyotelike grin of terror, his eyes bugged out and zoned over, and his idiotic exclamation: "Bro! It's cool, bro, you know my bro! You been to my house in Boise! You erped in my mom's closet! You know my bro!"

I never saw Carin Schlosser again, but I do have the indelible memory of her petite, well-tended vulvar presentation. I was escorted out of the dining hall that night by campus security. My dorm "friends" rifled through all my stuff the next day and robbed me blind.

TEN

HIT THE ROAD LITERALLY

WE WERE BOMBING down Highway 81, doing about 120 in Shane's Explorer, screaming at one another, smearing Pond's cold cream all over our faces to get the clown makeup off. I was yelling at Shane because he was such an asshole for adding "armed" to our robbery, and almost murder. But the other three jokers were totally jacked up, high-fiving like they'd won the Super

Bowl. Timbo started passing around the peyote, and for some reason, I downed a couple of buttons, enough to launch me for another twelve hours. I crumpled the Ziploc with a few more buttons in it and stuffed it in my pocket, getting back to the task of reaming Shane. The plan was that we'd drive to Portland, divide the money—me getting the lion's share for pulling the whole thing together—and go our separate ways, trying not to spend like lotto winners.

Timbo said from the back, "There's like forty-five fuckin' grand in here. Holy shit!"

"Yeah," added Shane, "and if it wasn't for me, you guys woulda been up shit creek."

"Can the fucking rafting talk, Shane," I said. "You almost accessorized us, you fuck."

"I created the diversion we needed to get outta there."

"And if I hadn't stopped you from shooting Baby? What, you don't really have murder in your heart?"

Shane slowed down to about thirty and looked away from his driving, looked me right in the eye. "Yeah, I got murder in my heart, Professor."

I felt Raol's arm lock around my neck, and then a bunch of liquid spilling down the front of my shirt.

"Raol, what the fuck," I said, scolding him for spilling his drink on me. Then the pain started, searing across my throat, and I saw my shirt blacking with blood. I jerked my head, twisting my jaw against Raol's arm.

"Oh, fuck. Oh, shit," Timbo said, shrinking away into the recesses of the backseat.

Shane reached over calmly and opened the passenger door, still doing about thirty.

Raol twisted my neck again, torquing me right out of the car, my knapsack twisting around me as I fell and rolled into the scrub. I took a hard hit on a road reflector that passed between my legs, clocking me in the balls so that briefly, all other pain was secondary. It felt like I must have somersaulted for fifty yards, but I'm sure the reality was less spectacular.

·

I LAY IN the dead quiet at the edge of the Columbia River Basin. Flecks of blood fogged my vision, but even so, I could see the night was beautiful. I slowly reached my hand to my throat. From what I could tell, the geniuses had missed their mark—the artery was intact.

But my neck had been sliced up pretty good. I felt a rush of warmth and giddiness, and I patted my bloodied shirt pocket. Sure enough, the Ziploc was there with the two remaining peyote nubs. I chewed them slowly and methodically, enjoying the horrible taste as a diversion from my other ills. I looked at the heavens; the moon was already on its descent through the untroubled sky.

ELEVEN

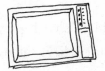

MY SLAVE

AT EIGHT-FORTY-FIVE I started rapping on Nik Slave's door, in full Johnny Delficcio regalia.

"Mr. Slave? Western Cable."

I wanted to catch Slave early, not that I expected him to be up at nine anyway. I knocked on the door a little longer, until I heard him rustling around. There were no other voices, just the sounds of one sleep-deprived person trying to put it together to get to the door for his freebie.

After more fumbling, Rick Dellard, aka Nik Slave, opened the door. He didn't make eye contact, just bobbed his head and turned away, his own personal brand of hospitality.

"Mr. Slave?" I said. "Could I get you to show me your unit? You wouldn't believe the responses I get to that one. Haw, haw!"

Again, he bobbed his head and moved toward his battered Panasonic, with a pair of crappy rabbit ears balanced precariously on top.

Looking at the new and improved Rick Dellard, I could hear his band to the very note. It would be a little bit Ratt, or Foreigner, or Foghat, the bands that all the new punks seemed to worship. But it would also be fetishy. They would wear uniforms, shorts and ties possibly, lots of mascara, and all their piercings and tats would be proudly displayed in a vague nod to glam.

I pretended to dick around with his TV while I scoped the place. He didn't recognize me at all, even though we had spent numerous nights partying at the Pit, an outdoor dirt bowl in the hills above Boise, where we had endless raves and bongathons.

Slave's apartment was the blue-plate poverty special; a couple of rooms with puked-on, puke-colored carpet, thin, stained stucco walls, cottage-cheese ceilings, and furniture pulled from garbage heaps.

Nik was collapsed on a shapeless futon couch, busy picking his nose, probably dislodging last night's crank boogers. I started to wander toward the back room, looking at a piece of cable.

"Hey, hey," he grunted, "why you gotta go back there?"

"Cableman's job is part detective work, Nik," I said, holding up the useless piece of cable. "Gotta follow this bitch till I find out where she goes."

"You look familiar," he said, lifting his head as high as I had seen it yet, which gave him the look of a foraging animal that had picked up a scent.

"You been around the neighborhood awhile, Mr. Slave?"

"Awhile."

"Well, I've been servicing the area for the past three years. Everybody knows Johnny Delficcio."

"Right . . . but I feel like . . . I *know* you."

"What, in the biblical sense?" I laughed a big Johnny Delficcio haw-haw-haw. "Now, how 'bout that coffee?"

"Coffee . . ."

"Milk, two sugars!" I bellowed, my cover now bordering on a bad Scooby-Doo episode. The more nervous I got, the more Johnny Delficcio howled and demanded to be called out. But Nik Slave, true to his new name, slumped into the kitchen and started banging pots.

I looked into the trashed-out bathroom. Nothing. I turned toward the bedroom, my hand on my tool belt.

Rising out of the bed, in her uniform of thong panties and a midriff KISS T-shirt, was Xana Calipatria.

"Bailey!"

MANGO

I put a finger to my lips and nodded toward the .22 at my hip. She put her hands in front of her as if to shoo me away.

"Where are they?" I asked.

"They think you're dead! I didn't tell them anything—"

"Yeah, right."

"I didn't. Especially . . ." She lifted up her KISS T-shirt and flashed the mangoes (now unbruised), and I was abruptly transported to happier times.

"You almost done?" Nik called from the other room.

"Three more minutes and you're golden, there, Nik," I said.

Xana and I looked at each other. She was wondering how much I'd believe, and I was wondering how much to believe. I honestly didn't know. I had the gun, but she had the bead on Shane and the money.

I threw my eyes in Nik Slave's direction. "He know anything?"

"Nothing."

"Where are they?" I asked again, playing the gun more prominently.

"I don't know. But they were here. And I'm pretty sure they'll be back."

"C'mon, Xana, you can do better than that."

I cocked the gun in her direction, but no way in hell was I about to shoot her. It was just what tough guys did in these situations, wasn't it?

"Bailey, no! Let me help you."

"How are you gonna help me?"

"I got you here, didn't I?"

I nodded, waiting for her to come up with a plan, because I had absolutely nothing. "You got me here, and I still don't see any sign of Shane and those other two assholes."

"I'll deliver them to you if you cut me in."

I shook my head. This chick was shameless. She was pouting, on her knees, waiting for my answer. The KISS T-shirt was still riding up from where she had flashed me.

I held up a hand, five fingers splayed. "Five grand," I said.

Her naughty-girl smile reappeared.

TWELVE

IT WORKS IF YOU WORK IT

I HAD TAKEN to walking around Venice and Santa Monica. I was way down on my cash supply, and the VW was a potential hazard if anyone decided to run the plates. Besides, a strange thing was happening. It had probably been since I was fourteen that I'd gone this long without drugs or alcohol, and I was a mess. But I couldn't face the thought of getting high. I felt like

Spider-Man or something, with constantly tingling Spidey senses. It wasn't superhero cool; I was jonesing. I finally understood the anguish Peter Parker must have felt after he'd been bitten by that radioactive spider. He wasn't happy about his gift; it kept him from leading a normal life like all the other students, and it was forever thwarting him from getting laid by Mary Jane, or whatever his girlfriend's name was.

My nerves were frayed live wires, and life was a giant puddle. The sun was too bright, the sky too blue, my clothes moved against my skin in disturbing undulations. Was this the process of coming down, or was I experiencing that feeling people are always trying to describe when they talk about Los Angeles? Nothing seemed to have any context, and I was in the middle of some kind of Schopenhauerian morass, struggling with my own free will.

The players were getting fuzzy for me. I kept forgetting that my own friends had tried to off me. And Xana? I had no idea what to make of her. She had thrown me a bang, she certainly had that in her favor, but she was Shane's chick, and they had been together awhile. On the other hand, Shane was an asshole, and I had offered her five grand to help me out. The money would win the day.

I was walking somewhere down by the beach, passing one Starbucks after another, when I heard a vaguely familiar voice say, "Boo." I hauled myself out of my funk to see Sissy, the beguiling wolf-eyed hooker. "Hey, homie," she said.

"Hey. Sissy, right?"

"You got it. Bailey."

I nodded. We looked at each other for a long moment, her bobbing her head and smiling that hippie-girl smile, me unable to look away from those eyes.

SCHOPENHAUER

"You never called me," she said.

"Yeah, been busy."

"That's cool."

We stood for another moment. It was that L.A. thing again. I couldn't quite get my eyes to focus against the glare.

"Dude, you look tweaked." She cocked her head slightly, as if that would put me right. "You wanna get that latte?" she asked, looking like she expected a resounding no.

"I'm sorry, I'm a little . . ." I gestured to my pockets.

"You got me on a good day," she said. "I am one rich bitch."

She took me down a side street to a place called Van Go's Ear, a divey beatnik coffee joint with a mixed bag of art on the walls and lots of intense artist-model-screenwriter types. She bought us each a big, nasty mocha, and we sat upstairs in an alcove. I had absolutely nothing to say. I just put my head in the coffee and hunkered over it like an asthma inhaler. She didn't seem to mind; she chattered on like I was a regular person or a regular trick. The thing that was wrong with the picture, though, was that she was buying me coffee and she knew I was broke. Unless she was working a long con on me. I decided to let her know I wasn't her guy.

"I'm sorry, y'know, that I can't give you any money."

"For the coffee?"

"Well, for . . . no, for whatever."

"For whatever?"

"Well, I'm taking up your working time."

"I'm not working now. How could I be?"

"Y'know, it's not like you're gonna get any customers while you're talking to me."

"Customers?" She looked at me as a long slow

dawning took place for both of us. "Wait," she said, "you think I'm working you? Like . . . a working girl?"

I stared in the lupine eyes, my tongue suddenly feeling salty and bloated. I looked away.

"Why would you . . . I mean, fuck. Fuck you. What is your fucking—"

"I . . . You asked me if I was a cop."

" 'Cause you looked lost. I figured you were lost or you were a cop. And I thought you were cute . . . Jesus. Either you got some woman issues, or I must really look like a Lincoln Boulevard crack whore."

"No," I sputtered, "the first thing—"

"You don't know me, Bailey, you don't *even* . . ." She held out a hand. "Try to read my palm."

I looked dumbly at her hand. It was rough, lined prematurely, like the hide of an exotic animal.

"You can't, right? All you can see is it looks like I've worked hard. Now read these."

She pushed up the sleeves of her surfer shirt. She had brutal, careless track marks, collapsed veins, the ruined arms of a career skin-popper. "Yeah, they're fucked up, huh? But look again: There ain't one track on these fuckers that's newer than three years old. That's my goddamn fortune—I'm clean. *Three years.* And look closer, I fuckin' bus tables at Ivy at the fuckin' Shore and I make my hundred bucks a night and I go home and I walk my ravenous fuckin' rottweiler who is the only living being in the universe I trust and I love."

My mouth seemed to be lined with metal. "I—I'm really—"

"No. No way. It ain't that easy."

I looked at her, her lips trembling and her voice full of emotion, the one person who had actually shown me any kindness since I crossed the California border. I looked away.

"You ever give anyone a cake, motherfucker?" she asked.

•

IT WAS JUST around the corner, a cinder-block community center painted poor-man brown. I was wedged against a far wall, and in order to escape, I would have to pass through a gauntlet of tattooed, embittered, vigilantly sober people. I'd always been of the opinion that the only thing more dangerous than an addict was someone who was sober, especially recently sober. They carried around those chips announcing how many months they hadn't been smoking, drinking, snorting, or shooting whatever substance had toppled them. It seemed like they were always looking for some crisis or conflict that would give them an excuse to go right back out and cop. Needless to say, I kept my head down, my shades on, and watched the proceedings like I belonged. Just like in the movies, people would stand up and say, "My name is Dickwad, and I'm an addict." People were uniformly compassionate and shouted out different slogans in such a way that I jumped every time somebody hollered, "It works if you work it! Keep coming back!"

They worked around the room, different people talking about their various stages of sobriety, about hitting "rock bottom," about feeling like they were "the piece of shit at the center of the universe."

When they got to Sissy, it was clearly a big deal. She looked over at me, and a small, sad-looking bald guy thrust a cake in my hands with three lit candles. Everyone sang "Happy Birthday" to her, and she really lit up, her smile for the first time unguarded and childlike. I walked the cake up to the front of the room, and she made her way to a thrashed podium, worked and worried by the sweaty palms of hundreds of sober junkies.

She thanked her friend Bailey for giving her the cake, and I felt like absolute crap. She started to give her testimonial, and I got to sit back down.

"I don't want to talk much," she said as everyone settled down for her to talk for a long time. "I just want to say that every day I have my sobriety is a blessing. And it's a weird blessing, because the second I start to lose sight of it, to take it for granted, then it threatens to overtake me and disappear. What I have to remember like the fucking stations of the cross is that I am a heroin addict and an alcoholic. And three years ago I was stealing from my friends and family, stealing from strangers and prostituting myself not two hundred feet from where we're sitting right now, so"—here she glanced over at me—"really you were closer than you might think. The real blessing is when that becomes a reality for me, when I remember without a junkie's nostalgia that I'm not just a sober busgirl at a fancy restaurant who can paint beautiful pictures. I'm a junkie, a thief, and a whore." On the last word she looked over at me again. I was still watching from under my shades.

I guess Sissy had been the grand finale, because after everybody clapped, the bald guy got up and made a few announcements. Then they all chanted something called the Serenity Prayer.

I felt it first oddly, in my shoulders, which bobbed up and down a few times in rapid succession. Then I felt a searing gasp rip through my lungs and the lowest reaches of my belly.

I was sobbing. I kept my head down, but it was all I could do not to bawl like a colicky infant. The meeting was breaking up, and luckily people were moving around, or they surely would have heard me gasping for breath. All of the insanity, the tough-guy posturing, slid away. I sat in the folding chair like a lost little kid.

I felt something solid on my back and realized someone was offering comfort. I looked up to see an enormous biker with a cutoff leather jacket bearing the insignia of some fearsome biker club. He patted me rhythmically, his catcher's mitt of a hand covering most of my back. He didn't smile or offer words of any kind, just looked at me with a sad deadpan, as if the knowing was enough.

THIRTEEN

Cancerous Horses and Psychotic Elephants

FOR THE MOST part, banality reigns at the circus. Being in almost any job at the circus is like playing goalie: long periods of sheer boredom interrupted by a second or two of sphincter-puckering danger.

In my tenure with the circus, I had seen it happen only a couple of times. Rolph, who worked with the big cats, called it "goink off all vocky," which I think meant "going off all wacky," but everyone imitated him with his thick Austrian accent, so I never did actually find out if "vocky" was a special word unique to Rolph's language or just his bad accent.

The first time I saw things go off all vocky, I was new to the circus—about two weeks in—and had been given the new-guy assignment of following the elephants around during the parade and trying to catch their massive shits before they hit the ground. I'd had just about enough of this assignment; the long-timers took great pleasure in watching the new guy in orange coveralls concentrating so hard on catching the mega-loads. When they give you this job, they tell you you've been assigned as the elephant trainers' apprentice, and then, of course, they have a big laugh watching you go from excitement to chagrin as they explain what the job entails.

So I was a shit catcher, and for a guy who's used to copping free, catching shit was some kind of horrible instant karma.

Before the parade in each show, I'd help the handlers bring the elephants out and wash them down. Circus Maximus was a three-ring big-top circus, actually the last of its type on the continent since Barnum & Bailey had moved into auditoriums and done away with the tent. Maximus also was a low-rent poor relation to Barnum and would buy their lower-quality animals at a big discount. So we got blind tigers, cancerous horses, psychotic elephants, and worked them literally to death.

There was no excuse for the way the trainers handled the elephants. They were big, smart, and generally kind beasts who were being asked to be humiliated eight shows a week. One elephant, Szabo, was a fairly recent purchase from Barnum & Bailey. Szabo was an African elephant, a bull male, and full of unknowns. The rumor was that Szabo had a mean streak, and even though nothing serious had happened over at Barnum, they were looking to unload the elephant before he went off all vocky.

The elephant trainers, Lloyd and Jose, were angry, smelly little dudes, both about five foot three, both thick through the middle, neckless, and shaved-headed.

A bull hook—the principal tool for handling an elephant—looks like a walking cane but is made out of heavy steel and is sharp on the hooked end. The handlers get the elephants to comply by reaching up with the hooked end and sinking it anywhere in the elephant's mouth area—almost like catching a fish—until the big mammal goes where the handler wants.

It's something to see these giant beasts, who are so sophisticated that they bury and mourn their dead, being led around like cattle. Every once in a while one of the bulls has an awareness of how big, how powerful, how potentially deadly he can be. Szabo had one of these elephant existential moments while Jose was working him, trying to get him out of the watering area and in line for the parade. Elephants dig water, and for circus elephants, water is the only pleasure they have left, other than getting an occasional sniff of the ass of the elephant in front of them.

Szabo wanted to stay in the water for a while, and when Jose slapped the bull hook up into his mouth, Szabo reared a little, no big deal. Jose repositioned the bull hook, bore down, and twisted. The twist was unnecessary and caused Szabo to do something elephants rarely do: He batted Jose away with a flick of his trunk, a tiny gesture that lifted Jose into the air and onto his ass in a nanosecond.

The air got very thick as Jose looked up at Szabo looking down with a new perspective, of size and power.

Just as Szabo's worldview had shifted, so had Jose's. He was looking up from a small and powerless place. He was a human, slow and clumsy, and weak as the rest of us. He had been stripped of his tools. All of a sudden he was a cowering *Australopithecus*.

Szabo started prancing with his massive front legs, raking Jose's flailing arms and legs. Then he scooped the handler up with his trunk and body-slammed him over and into the bloody asphalt, to the point where I noticed the yellow parking lines were no longer visible in that area.

Nobody made a move to save Jose during Szabo's rampage—including me—until finally, when it was over and Jose lay in an unrecognizable heap on the asphalt, the other trainer, Lloyd, disappeared for a moment. The air was still, charged with the strange magic of violence, but Szabo, having shot his wad, stood there panting and looking quietly distracted.

Lloyd ran back into the wash area with a thirty-aught-six, an elephant gun, which was supposed to be at the ready to prevent the kind of thing that had just happened. Lloyd walked right up to the bull and leveled off the rifle, firing point-blank at Szabo, who took two bullets and keeled over like a felled cedar.

Lloyd looked around as if there might be more takers for the gun. Then he lowered it and fell to his knees and started bawling.

In retrospect, judging by their matching hairdos, body types, and wardrobes, it makes sense that Lloyd was lamenting the loss of his lover, though homosexuality was rarely directly acknowledged in the circus (it would be seen as a weakness to exploit). It's also possible that Lloyd was mourning the loss of Szabo, his biggest and most handsome elephant. His grief was that large and vague.

Given what I had seen, there was a lot to be amazed and horrified by. But all I could do was marvel at Lloyd's immediate access to his emotion, his connection to the repercussions of what he had experienced only seconds earlier. I turned and walked back toward the riggers' bunks. Work would be delayed at least an hour.

FOURTEEN

THE THIRD CHAIR

ONCE AGAIN, I was sitting in Nik Slave's back alley in the last affordable beach community in Southern California. Every so often a homeless guy would come along and nose around in the trash, or a carload of *vatos* would lowride by, watching me watch them.

This was the moment. They were meeting at Slave's on their way over to their big buy. But I wasn't going to let the buy go down. I knew those ningnods would probably wind up with forty grand worth of nothing.

I would get a window signal from Xana, who would also make sure Shane's weapons were temporarily unloaded. Then I'd move in.

It was a tough place to keep an eye on. It was on what they call a walk street, the front entrance on a pedestrian-only promenade, just the rear alley accessible by car. As far as I could tell, only tourists and skateboarders used the pedestrian paths, and all the traffic happened in the alleys. Written on the side of the building, along with the usual ghetto gang tags, were the gigantic bold-printed words EXEUNT TODO MYSTERIUM, which meant, I was shocked to remember from my two semesters of Latin, "All things go forth in mystery."

My plan was simple. After I accosted my old pals, I would take the cash and pull out my share, plus a tengrand fine for the attempted murder and inconvenience. I would tell them that to pursue me would only cause them unhappiness, even death. I would back out of the place, get in my stolen vehicle, and take a circuitous route back east, never to set foot on West Coast soil for the rest of my days.

I didn't have the stomach for murder, especially after

my little come-to-Jesus at the A.A. meeting. I just wanted out of this place, with its boardwalk full of shattered Vietnam vets and psychics, its obsession with beauty, and its voracious appetite for gasoline and power. But here I was, thinking about Sissy's heartbreaking testimonial, her piercing eyes, her simultaneous accusation and acquittal of my unforgivable behavior.

When Shane's Explorer pulled into the alley, I had a brief physical memory of my last trip in the vehicle, my nutsack contracting reflexively. I watched them pile out, Timbo and Raol following behind Shane like a couple of Sherpas.

It was supposed to be a matter of five or ten minutes before I got the signal from Xana. I made sure I was locked and loaded, and went over the floor plan in my head. Everything seemed to be in order.

Ten minutes passed. Fifteen. Forty. At one point I thought I saw a bright light issue from the window, and I thought I might be hearing some kind of noise from the place. But it was hard to tell with the traffic.

Finally, about an hour in, I tucked the .22 into the back of my belt and quietly worked my way up the stairs.

The door was slightly open, and I found myself suddenly doing an *NYPD Blue*, the ridiculous gun drawn professionally, as if I knew what I was doing. My own actual firearm experience was limited to a drunken weekend of chucker hunting in Idaho, during which Doug Oram had inadvertently shot himself in the leg, shattering his tibia and fibula.

I pushed open the door slightly, enough so I could slip inside. I held the gun in front of me, gritting my teeth, my eyes all but squeezed shut.

First was the smell, overwhelming and sulfurous, intimate. Two chairs. No, three. Two people sitting in chairs. For a second I thought they were looking up at something of great interest on the ceiling. I actually glanced up.

Then I saw that it was Timbo and Raol, their throats cut wide open and notched, creating a grotesque caricature of an ear-to-ear grin: a

ROAD FLARE

wide, toothless mouth that gave them the appearance of slaughtered Muppets. Inside each notched opening, shoved deep into their windpipes, was the charred remnants of a flare, exactly like the roadside flares we had used to rip off the payroll. Their necks were blacked with carbon and burned blood where the flare had played out its life. From the expressions on their tipped-back heads, Timbo and Raol had been alive for some of this. I remembered Arnold's threat to me back at the circus, and I knew that Timbo and Raol were only the appetizers. I would be the main course.

The third chair was empty. An unused flare sitting on it. This would be mine. My stomach flipped, and I clutched the gun tight. I backed toward the door, then took a quick look at Nik Slave's hellhole.

I could see through into the bedroom. Something looked odd about the futon on the floor. I moved toward it. At first I was going to start shooting, then check, but since I had hardly ever fired a gun, I kicked it first and heard a frightened gasp. I kicked the futon back, ready to fire. Xana Calipatria lay there, trembling, trying to breathe.

"No . . . no . . . no, please," she whimpered.

I lowered the gun. "What happened? Where's Shane?"

"He got away. I think."

A sickness was welling up in me, an overwhelming, crushing nausea.

"I don't know. I was hiding. They . . . I don't know. I

feel like there's no way I could have seen what I thought I saw . . ."

"What did you see?" I asked.

"I was under the futon . . . I could only see . . . this—I don't know—*thing*. On a skateboard. Like a person, but not . . . She was laughing. And some freak with tattoos all over his face . . . and I could hear Timbo and Raol . . . What happened?"

I picked her up from the floor. "You don't want to know," I said.

I grabbed her by the arm and dragged her next to me like a sack of laundry. I shielded her from Timbo and Raol as we passed.

"What was that—what happened?" she asked.

We stumbled together down the stairs. When we came out from the overhang, the California sun was blinding.

FIFTEEN

A DANGEROUS ERECTION

THE THING ABOUT Eelie was how smart she was, how self-deprecating and intelligent, how she'd say one thing and let a hundred other things float to the surface, batting them around like a cat playing with a wounded mouse and saving something for later. So it was surprising to me when she fell for my advances. But she did, at least by all appearances. I'd figure out her comings and goings and plan to run into her on the way to or from the show on those rare instances she wasn't with Arnold. She'd always look surprised, then immediately suppress it and give me her charming, tight-lipped smile (which wasn't really a smile at all, more like a half-grimace). The effect her smile had on me was to make me want to see more of it, to make it real.

WE BOTH KNEW, without ever acknowledging it or voicing it in any way, that there was no reason the two of us should be together, and that the first order of business was to invent some reason to be inordinately close. Without actually making a plan together, we solved that one in almost no time.

The second time I bumped into Eelie, I walked with her while she moved along on her skateboard, struggling to maintain both her balance and dignity in the course of the strange locomotions necessary for her to move the thing along. When we got back to her trailer, I eyed the system that had been set up for her to help herself inside.

"So how does this thing work?" I asked.

"Piss-poorly," she said, scowling at the poorly designed hand pull that she couldn't quite operate. "I don't really even use it, except in emergencies, when I can't get someone to help me inside. Even then I usually just wait around till somebody comes by."

"Well," I said, "rigging is my business these days. Maybe I could come up with something better."

The smile again, just a flicker before it dove down out of sight. "You think?" she asked. "That's a lot of work."

I shrugged. "Keep me outta trouble."

A little more of the smile. I could tell she wanted to say something about trouble, but she let it pass. "We could pay you," she offered.

"I don't think so. Anyway, I might end up doing a lousy job."

But I knew I wouldn't. I could have access to the full rigging shop.

"You look like a boy with a good Protestant work ethic," she said, with the barest trace of irony in her voice.

"Looks can be deceiving."

"Mmm." She looked up at me from her skateboard and moved a flipper in my direction. "Take me up to paradise, will ya?"

I picked her up and she smiled again, uncomfortable but seeming to enjoy it some. I carried her up the steps and inside. The trailer appeared darker and more depressing than it had the first time. Arnold's filthy clothes were everywhere, and the smell of his lighter-fluid funk permeated everything except Eelie herself, who smelled of freesia and baby powder.

When I moved to set her down on her bed, I lost my balance and we ended up side by side, my arm draped over her to keep my weight off her.

"Oops," I said.

"Hello."

"Hi. Sorry."

"No apology necessary."

We were face-to-face, looking right at each other, maybe four inches apart. I kissed her. It wasn't so much a part of my master plan as something I wanted to do at that moment. Eelie flushed as soon as the kiss broke, looking briefly into my eyes, then casting them down.

"You better run along before my husband comes in and douses you with gasoline," she said, giving a mirthless laugh.

I nodded and backed toward the door. "So I'll make up a couple of drawings. For the trailer."

"Right."

"Uh, okay. Cool. Thanks."

"Look," she said, her frankness already clearing the air. "I'm going to pay you for the work."

Before I could protest, she hushed me with the shrug of an appendage and continued. "Money is my arena around here. If Arnold has a problem with you being here, he'll have less to say about it if it's a financial matter."

I nodded, smoothing the covers where I had messed them up.

"Kiss me again," she said. "And touch me."

I kissed her again, running a hand tentatively over where her shoulder would have been if she had one. Sliding over that spot, I touched one of her flippers, right alongside a breast. I paused there, cupping the fullness of her, and was suddenly in a zone of normalcy. Her tits were actually beyond normal: They were exceptional. She was expressive but not desperate with her mouth, receiving me with a kind of neutrality that was both expert and near clinical and drove me absolutely crazy.

I had the uncomfortable realization that being with Eelie Willow was thrilling not just because her husband might light me on fire, or because I stood to get the inside dope on the payroll, but because being with Eelie Willow was exciting in and of itself. She was, strangely, the fulfillment of some essential male fantasy. She was an object to be objectified while being a person as well. She was physically not unlike a blow-up doll or a rubber vagina, in that she required a partner to move her, line her up, and make the act in any way possible. Yet she was, in parts, an attractive and intelligent woman who talked, participated in foreplay, and murmured appreciatively at all the right moments. I was as attracted to her as I had ever been to anyone.

We kept kissing and touching; something was getting close to happening when I heard the sound of voices outside the trailer. I stood up quickly, willing the pup tent in my jeans to fold itself up for the day. Eelie darted her eyes toward a beat-up easy chair in the corner, and I sat unnaturally in it, perching on the edge as the voices grew louder. Now I could make them out more distinctly. It was Arnold and Baby. My cock, brazenly disobeying orders from headquarters, refused to retreat to a more defensive position. I was about to be done in by my own hard-on.

Eelie said in a calm tone, "So, when do you think

you can have some drawings ready?" Her eyes darted over to me again.

"Oh . . . well . . . I think . . . maybe three or four days. A week at the most," I said too loudly.

The conversation outside the trailer stopped.

Eelie continued on about the drawings. "Okay, well, I'll give you a hundred for the plans, and if that works out, then—"

Arnold threw the door open, immediately assessing the situation. He was sweating and, for whatever reason, as filthy as an oil-rig worker.

"No problem," I said, doing my best to make it seem that Arnold's presence was in no way unexpected.

"Hey," he said, addressing either both of us or neither of us.

"Hey," answered Eelie. I just nodded. Thankfully, the flag was now flying stubbornly at half-mast. I only needed a few more moments to be out of the erection zone.

"Honey, this fellow here works in props and rigging."

"Yeah, I seen him," said Arnold, waiting to see if there was any more information coming before he kicked my ass.

"What was your name again?" Eelie asked. She was Frigidaire cool, and I wanted her bad.

"Bailey . . . Quinn."

"Right. Mr. Quinn here saw me trying to get inside the trailer, and he said he might be able to rig up something that actually works to get me up here on my own."

Arnold's eyes narrowed as he considered this. He licked some grease from his sweaty upper lip.

"Okay," I said inappropriately. "I'll see you guys later."

As I made my way outside, Arnold followed me to the bottom step of the trailer. Baby and Bezio stood off to the side, arms folded identically in the universal posture of the efficient killer, looking like absurd Secret Service men. Bezio's tats ranged from recent and professional to old prison ink, blurred and keloided beyond recognition. The one that always got me was that pair of rotting werewolf or mummy hands around his neck.

"You gonna give us a good deal?" Arnold asked. He smiled in a hopeful and boyish way. I could only assume this was some type of flirtation face he used for negotiations.

"Oh, sure," I said, trying to smile back.

Arnold's smile vanished as quickly as it had appeared. He stepped down off the trailer and got uncomfortably close. His breath smelled like some description of dragon's breath I had once read in a fantasy novel: like fiery, rotting death.

"If I see you carryin' my wife around, I'm gonna know what's what." He raised his eyebrows suggestively. Even as guilty as I already was, I think a look of genuine puzzlement crossed my face. Arnold elucidated, "You fuck around with my little Eelie, I'm gonna tear off your head and light a fire in your neck."

This was an odd variation on I-wouldn't-piss-down-your-throat-if-your-guts-were-on-fire, but it bore the timbre of a genuine threat.

I smiled thinly at Arnold, my throat suddenly parched, and got on my board, kicking through the maze of trucks back toward my tiny bunk.

SIXTEEN

THE IVY, WITH RESERVATIONS

IN LOS ANGELES, there's a sense of artificiality that extends even to sunsets. As I hustled Xana down the sidewalk on Ocean Boulevard, the sky was filled with a winking, lurid tequila sunset, the deep grenadine red at the bottom wavering like a backdrop that had been nudged by a careless stagehand. I held her firmly by the elbow and hustled her along. She stumbled and I caught her.

"OhGodohGodohGodohGod . . . Bailey, was that real? What we saw? Was that . . . oh God . . ."

"Shut up," I said. It was all I could offer in the way of comfort.

"Stop!" she shrieked.

I ducked and moved off the sidewalk, pulling her with me. But I could see she'd gone to some slightly crazy place. She was smiling drunkenly out at the ocean.

"Look at that!" she gasped.

"Yeah, the sunsets always look good here. It's the smog."

"No," she insisted. "Look."

I looked out toward Santa Monica Bay, down off the unsteady Palisades. A huge pod of dolphins was rhythmically arcing through the water, breaking the smooth surface into a quarter mile of undulating movement, like a rug weaving itself.

"They're so beautiful," she said. I decided to let her have her one second of escape. The road ahead was looking pretty nasty.

We stood there looking out at the water, watching

the dolphins thread their way south. To a passerby, we might have looked like a couple of tourists taking in the pacific wonders of the Southern California sunset: ordinary, even serene. A siren wailed and put me immediately back in my body. I pulled on Xana's arm and steered us across the street.

My worldview, founded almost entirely on my steadfast belief in copping free, had been completely shattered with one look at Timbo and Raol, sitting in their chairs, gazing stupidly at the cottage-cheese ceiling of Nik Slave's sad apartment. Any thought I may have had of getting my money back, my college nest egg, was blown wide open. Now I'd be lucky to leave L.A. with my life.

COPPING FREE WAS no longer an illusion that I could foster in the hope of convincing myself I was not just another lowlife criminal sociopath, an animal pretending to walk on two legs. My naïve commitment to harmless felonies was gone, a thing of the past, and any action I took now would be with the full knowledge that it could ripple through and shatter the lives of others.

Even as I pondered this, I headed toward the one person I had encountered in Los Angeles who had not been affected by my stupidity.

I slammed through the doors of Ivy at the Shore like I belonged there, or like I was about to announce a tidal wave headed straight for the place. Nobody at the bar or in the waiting area noticed me, but the maître d' scoped me before I could avoid him and rushed over as if he were the only one who had noticed my pants were down around my ankles.

"Hi! How are you?" I said.

He looked around to make sure I was talking to him. He was a good-looking guy with an almost comical Dudley Do-Right chin. He had probably been an actor or model when he came to Los Angeles, but now he was a lifer in the restaurant business. I had noticed a bunch of these types. They always looked bewildered, with an air of bitterness wafting around them, like they'd been stuck on some prison work program. It was either this or a denialfest of missionary zeal about their newly chosen line of work—the latter description fitting our Dudley Do-Right—that manifested itself in a kind of mania.

"Good evening," Dudley groaned, his teeth clenched

in an uncomfortable smile. "Do you have reservations?" He looked from me to his reservation book, knowing there would be no match.

What had tipped Dudley off that I was not to be dining at his establishment on this particular evening? Was it my clothes? Maybe. But as I glanced at the bar, I saw a few other guys dressed about as casually. Was it my age? Most of the patrons were thirties and older, but that couldn't be it; surely young Hollywood dined at the Ivy on occasion. For all Dudley knew, I was one of them, a drug-addled young actor with a sitcom deal. Was it . . . I did the math.

It was my eyes. They were wild. With fear, with rage, with shock. After racing out of Nik Slave's place, I had come to the only place where I might get to see someone who wasn't out to get me. I was crazed, and Dudley Do-Right knew it, and he knew that it was a primary objective of his new career, since he gave up his dream of getting a shot on *Friends,* to show me the door.

"You don't remember me, do you?" I asked.

"Excuse me?" Dudley, God bless him, was still working to keep that smile from collapsing onto his absurdly cleft chin.

"From that class?" I figured he must have taken some kind of classes in L.A. somewhere. Isn't that what these guys do? They move from whatever state it is where they grow people who look like this and bide their time taking classes until their big break comes along, or until they wake up one day as an assistant manager.

"Wait . . . Larry Moss?"

"No—Bailey."

"Larry Moss's *class*?"

"Right! Mossie!"

His eyes narrowed. I had gone out on a limb with the Mossie thing, and it had snapped.

"I used to call him that as a joke, remember? Pissed him off."

"No, I don't . . ." He leaned over conspiratorially. "I was so fucked up back then. Acting." He shook his head, sadder-but-wiser, to show me he had moved past his youthful folly.

"Yeah. Acting." I aped his head shake.

"You still going out on auditions?" he asked.

I was only vaguely aware that an audition was the humiliation an actor had to suffer in order to get a part.

The more successful I seemed, I figured, the more likely Dudley would be to let me in the door.

"Auditions? Sure."

"Booked anything?"

Was that good or bad? To book something? Had to be good. "Yeah. Totally."

"Great. Working now?" Dudley was taking the bait. Impressed but jealous. Would he punish me for succeeding when he had failed?

"Oh . . . just . . . this movie with Robert Downey, Jr."

Wait. Was he in jail? No. Good.

". . . and Tom Cruise and Helen Hunt."

I had shot my wad in terms of Hollywood names. I could feel a virulent sweat prickling the back of my shirt.

"Wow. Downey. And they insured him?"

"Wasn't easy. Great guy. Very sweet. Fucked up." I nodded sadly, hoping to crush the conversation.

"What's it called?"

My mind careened. *"Ghost . . ."*

Shit. That was taken.

". . . Chimp."

"*Ghost Chimp?*"

I nodded sickly. Where were all the customers?

"*Ghost Chimp,*" chortled Dudley. "Very clever. Very funny."

"Oh, yeah. Very. But also . . . moving." Why didn't I shut up?

"Huh." Dudley was preparing to be moved. He bowed his head.

"Oh, yeah. Downey—Robert—plays a brilliant but tortured animal trainer . . . who . . . loses his best friend."

"The chimp."

"*Right.*"

"So who does Cruise play?"

"The . . . chimp."

"Tom Cruise plays a chimp?" This one was about to crash.

"*After* . . . the chimp is reincarnated in the guise of . . . a *boxer*."

"Dog?"

"What?"

"A boxer dog?"

"No. Although . . . interesting."

"Right. A *boxer*."

"Who teaches Robert . . . to love again."

"Wow. Wow."

We took a moment.

"It's a powerful piece," I said.

"Who does Helen Hunt play?"

"A tough but ultimately vulnerable psychotherapist."

"Right, of course," said Dudley, as if this should have been obvious from the get-go. "And you?"

"Oh . . . I play . . . It's not a huge part."

"Nice . . . nice. I think I remember you from class."

Dudley was mine.

We both stood there nodding. An enormous group of people came in, all wearing what appeared to be the same expensive black leather coat. Dudley remembered his new calling and hopped to.

"Good evening!" he chirped. These were clearly Ivy at the Shore people. I looked at their eyes, full of a practiced flatness.

I stood by the waiter's station as Sissy came in with an armful of plates. She slid them into the bus tray and moved to get past me.

"Hey, Sissy."

She jumped when she saw it was me. "Jesus. What are you doing here?"

I tried to say something, to form a sentence, but nothing came out. I breathed in sharply and realized I was shaking pretty hard.

"Are you high?"

"No, no . . . not high."

I was hanging on to her arm so she wouldn't leave the waiter's station. But even more, I was holding on to her eyes. They bore neither the wild shock of mine nor the studied boredom of the Ivy patrons. They were as clear and sad and blue as Arctic ice water. She was wearing busgirl garb, black pants and a white shirt, but she looked beautiful and ordered. I desperately wanted a small amount of her equilibrium.

"I need help," I said at last.

I noticed she was looking over my shoulder. I glanced back to see Xana standing inside the door, shifting unsteadily from one foot to the other.

"What kind of help?" Sissy looked ready to dig into her pocket for some money. But how could I explain the kind of help I needed? I needed her sanity, her clarity—I needed to lie down next to her and find calm in her stillness.

"I need a place to stay," I said. "Just for a day or two."

She nodded, made an immediate decision she

seemed to regret just as she took out a set of keys and laid them solemnly in my hands. "Don't fuck up."

"I already have."

"Then don't fuck up more. You know where Brooks Avenue is?"

I shook my head.

"What *do* you know?"

"I know you look hot in your busgirl outfit."

She rolled her eyes. "Yeah. You and my lecherous boss. How are you with dogs?"

"I like 'em. Most of the time."

"Well, my dog can see right into your heart. You understand?"

"You mean, after he rips it out of my chest?"

"No. He's very special. If you're fucking with me, he'll know."

"Wow. Have you ever thought of exploiting his talents for profit?"

"I gotta go. Three-twenty-five Brooks."

SEVENTEEN

THE SCALLOP-SHAPED PILLOW

AFTER MY DAD stepped out on my mom, things went back to normal, like I said. But it was all too normal, too ordered, like a still life of a family. My dad, who had always been a party animal, started coming home at five-thirty and doing a pretty fair impression of a father. He'd pull off his tie, lay his jacket across the car, and throw a ball with me and my brother, or talk me into helping him make supper. Because he seemed to be acting like a father, I felt the need to act like a son, aping *Leave It to Beaver* reruns, being extra cheerful, smiling until my jaws ached, making kidlike jokes and saying corny son-to-dad-type stuff.

I watched my parents carefully when they interacted, looking for cracks in the façade. Although I often felt they were on the verge of slipping up, they got their lines right and did their movements. So I took to spying on them, sure that if I caught them in an unguarded moment, they would give something up that would reveal the hoax. I listened through the crack under the door as they talked about their days, moved in and out of their various uniforms, even as they dutifully fucked once every two weeks.

My mother had changed, but I couldn't put my finger on exactly how, almost as if in becoming more deeply herself, she was revealing her essential dishonesty. She still obsessed over the house, even to the point of stylish, modern redecorating, including brilliant white carpets, in denial of the two cats, the dog, and the two filthy boys. She ordered obscure but expensive Scandinavian and German furniture, turning the house slowly into an austere, neo-Bauhaus museum.

Some of the pieces she bought were on order for months and months. I imagined teams of hip foreign men laboring over our coffee table, our birch-veneer partitions, our slate-gray pigskin chaise longue.

My father, who used to gripe endlessly every time my mom bought asparagus, was conspicuously silent as she decorated us into bankruptcy. Every time a new piece arrived, a pair of geriatric turtlenecked men would carefully unload and polish the new acquisition. My father would come home from work, do a brief stutter step as he noticed it, and move on.

After a year of carpeting, painting, and arranging, the house was almost done. My mom was waiting on only one more piece, the coup de grâce, a large, unconstructed textile that would be draped dramatically across the couch. I was out riding my bike when the big square of fabric arrived.

I walked in the house and was immediately struck by the living room. My mom was right. Even to a ten-year-old of limited experience and taste, I could see, in the gently diffused light of a few carefully chosen lamps, that our house was as beautiful, as perfect, as any space I had ever seen. I walked over to the couch and touched the fabric. It was soft and inviting, textured. I stood and bathed in the light of my mother's obsession. Magazines would want to photograph the look, people would want her to re-create it for their homes, neighbors would jealously discuss it. But it would never be more perfect than at this moment, empty, untainted, void of associations.

I went to look for her, thinking of her now as something like a celebrity.

I looked in the bedroom, the den, out by the pool, calling to her. I opened the bathroom door, already ajar, and saw my mother.

Her head was resting against a scallop-shaped bath pillow, her dark curls cascading down in the water. For a moment I thought she had fallen asleep in a mineral bath, because the water was a thin Kool-Aid red. Her dark nipples rested at water level, and her mouth was slightly open, as if she were about to make a minor interjection.

•

IN THE WEEKS following my mother's funeral, my father dismantled the elaborately decorated interior of the house, sending back whatever he could, selling off the other pieces for a fraction of their value. I would be the only one to experience my mother's masterpiece as it was meant to be seen: simple, uninflected, private, filled with sadness and longing.

EIGHTEEN

A BEAUTIFUL CAR CRASH

I HAD PRETTY specific instructions from Sissy. Apparently the dog would accept me if I spoke clearly and called him by his name, Mocus. And if I fed him the enormous piece of leftover prime rib Sissy had slipped me.

I opened the side gate to Sissy's small bungalow, Xana following behind me, quiet as a geisha, and immediately heard a wet, throaty woofing. I walked up to the door, where Mocus was hurling himself repeatedly, a fleshy, slobbering battering ram.

"Mocus," I said, too full of false cheer. If I were Mocus, I'd have wanted to eviscerate me, too. He paused for a second, then resumed his assault on the door.

"Mocus. I'm your new friend," I said hopefully. I worked my way around to a window to look inside.

I've seen plenty of rottweilers before. Sure, they're the big, bad, macho dog du jour. So I'd been expecting big. But Mocus surpassed any notion I ever had of what his breed could be. He was half again as big as any rottweiler I'd ever seen. His head looked like a crudely chiseled cinder block, and his body was crazily muscled; he was a perfect and uncomplicated killing machine.

"Hey, buddy," I said. "Hey, Mocus, my name is Bailey, and I'm a friend of Sissy's. I have the keys."

I jingled the keys, and Mocus stopped barking altogether. I tried to breathe evenly, but I was coming to the realization that I was covered with a thick, greasy sheen of fear sweat. Dogs could smell fear like I could smell a barbecue.

I put the key in the door. It was quiet. I heard a

mockingbird calling urgently a block or two away. After surviving a murder attempt by my best friends, I wasn't about to let a rottie kill my buzz.

"Okay, Mocus . . ." I opened the door and braced myself. But the silence continued. Mocus was nowhere in sight.

Just as I took my first breath in five minutes, Mocus came bounding around the corner, grimacing silently and readying himself for the kill. I stepped to the side like a toreador and held out the rare and quivering prime rib. Mocus laid on the brakes.

"Mocus!" I said stupidly.

Mocus sat, suddenly my bitch. I gave him half the prime rib, withholding the rest in case he started acting up again.

I found his food and filled up his bowl, freshened his water, rubbed his unnaturally large head. At this point, he almost leered at me; we were homies.

Xana crept slowly in behind me. Mocus didn't have any problem with her; he just jammed his nose in her crotch and looked up at her expectantly.

Sissy's small guest-house-type bungalow, though it was located dead in the middle of a crack block, was not at all depressing. It was carefully furnished with thrift-store couches, castaways, and other found objects in an incredibly comforting and tasteful way. I wandered around picking things up: an old collection of classics and self-help books. A park bench had been sawed off at the backrest and covered with a piece of glass to make a coffee table. Mocus had fallen asleep on his bed.

I moved a curtain aside, revealing a small second bedroom that had been converted into a studio. Inside were dozens of completed canvases and several partially completed. I turned on a couple of halogen work lights. Unlike the cozy, lived-in bungalow, the studio space was ascetic and barren of everything except gesso, paint, brushes, stretchers, and canvas. The spartan studio felt like a place of ritual, a pathway to some other realm.

I sat on a small wooden chair, the only piece of furniture in the studio, and looked at the paintings. They were all depictions of car crashes, painted in rich, super-saturated color. The crashes were set on the bland, endless highways of Los Angeles, brightly colored cars engulfed in the vibrant reds and oranges of explosive fire. The finished canvases were worried, worked, and sanded, full of obsessive impastos, especially in the explosion areas. I sat in front of the paintings while Xana wandered through the other rooms, oohing and aahing over the décor. I looked at every painting, searching for some kind of message, some encoded clue, some sign to point me in a direction that would not end in death or in the finalization of my moral and literal bankruptcy. Even though the paintings moved me in a way art rarely did, they didn't provide any answers.

Finally I walked out of the studio into the living room, where Xana had passed out on the couch. I found a blanket and put it over her. By bringing her with me, I had increased the odds of being found, being killed, being tortured in a similar or even more gruesome way than my ex-friends had been tortured. Was it as simple and predictable as Xana's showing me the kindness of a mercy fuck? Or was I responding to her humanity? Was I reaching out to another lost soul in a strange land?

I looked down at her, simple and untroubled. She slept with the abandon and guilelessness of a small child.

I looked around for another place to rest, and all I could find was Sissy's bed, so I pulled a Goldilocks and rested uncomfortably in the corner of the bed, planning to take a catnap so I could wake up before Sissy's shift ended. The second I lay down, I was beset by crazy vertiginous images of the Freaks.

Whether they were dreams or alpha-state hallucinations, I'm not sure. I was lying on a banquet table, my limbs surrounded by roasted potatoes and my back and ass sunk in a hot, greasy gravy. Arnold sat at the head of the table, facing Eelie. Around the sides of the table were Baby and Bezio. They all wore lobster bibs and began cutting off large chunks of my flesh, smacking their lips and making exaggerated dining gestures.

Eelie had arms and ate of my body in enormous, gluttonous mouthfuls. I was disappointed that my meat was so easy; I was as pale and tender as a veal calf.

NINETEEN

ŞEND IN THE ŦUCK-YOU CLOWNS

I STARTED THINKING I might be the sensitive, artistic type after Bug, a rigging jock with Popeye forearms, held me down, pulled off my work gloves, and showed my hands to the crew. He knelt on my chest, and as I looked up at his prematurely jowled undercarriage, he held tightly to my uncalloused hands, hooting and shouting, "Check it out! The professor's hands are like, *pink*!"

After my humiliation with the props and rigging crew, I started thinking about other departments. Security, too boring; concessions, too mindless and low-paying . . . clowns.

Clowns, in the circus caste system, are a separate entity from crew and performers. Clowns tend to stay in their own clique, often traveling between a few different circuses, or taking it solo and busking in malls. It was a journeyman skill I could learn and take anywhere, although I found it a little pathetic, putting on a bunch of pancake makeup and behaving like an asshole. But the pay was double props and rigging, and really, how hard could it be?

The clowns at Maximus were a strange lot, drab and unremarkable without their makeup, and even in their makeup—their happy, smiley clown makeup—they could communicate a level of hostility I had rarely encountered. They were known to the crew as the Fuck-You Clowns.

The Fuck-You Clowns were a daunting phalanx, and the corner of the lot they occupied was theirs and theirs alone. I began to shadow them, carefully studying their act and their movements. The boss of the Fuck-You Clowns was a small, surly alcoholic named Darryl who did solo work with his raggedy-ass dog, about the size of a Jack Russell terrier but of no particular breed. They went by the mildly pretentious stage names of Pequin and Pepin, and I could never remember who was which. Under the big top, they had a great rapport, the dog jumping up and nipping at Darryl's butt every time he turned around, snatching the steering wheel from his little car, pulling a lever that caused him to go tumbling into a vat of water. Offstage, Darryl would get drunk and kick the dog's ass all over the lot. The abuse and invective were constant; you could hear them coming around the corner of the trailers by the curses and yelps. The dog, Pequin or Pepin, was desperate for love and food and attention, and Darryl was as stingy as any jailer. He doled out the barest modicum of affection during their act, when he would pop freeze-dried liver treats in the dog's mouth and pat him mechanically on the head after the successful completion of a trick.

The rest of the Fuck-You Clowns were a rank bunch of speed snorters and pot smokers, and their act was tired. Many of them, not unlike the Maximus elephants and big cats, were rejects from Barnum and bore the funk of the also-ran. Their skits were the most standard: They would pile out of a car, try to fix it, get back in; they would all try to extract a tooth from an unwilling dental patient, and so on.

I figured if the timing was right, I could get in with the Fuck-You Clowns and double my pay, kick back, and simultaneously be feared and protected, never to face a humiliation like the Bug episode again.

So I learned the clown moves, practicing secretly in dark corners of the big top, watching each part and deciding what role best suited me, the Dental Patient, the Crime Victim, the Driver, the Juggler.

When one of the Fuck-You Clowns was getting ready to leave the act to join a small family circus, I seized my opportunity. I talked to Darryl and told him I'd been working on the various sketches, that I'd love the chance to audition. He seemed interested, nodding as I flattered him and his troupe. He made an "O" with his mouth and jammed a Marlboro into it.

"Yeah, okay," he said. "Come by tonight after the last show. You can show us your moves." He smiled crookedly and exhaled smoke at me.

That night I was nervous as hell. My extremities were freezing, my breath was shallow, but I had the moves and I could stick the landing. I had even incorporated my skateboard into my routine. I was born to be a Fuck-You Clown.

Darryl waved me into the clown trailer. I immediately felt something was not right. It was just Darryl, the dog, and two of the Fuck-You Clowns. They were lounging around in their underwear, still sweaty from the show, cold cream streaking their hairlines.

"First we should come up with makeup for you," said Darryl, glancing at one of the other clowns, who nodded blankly. They sat me down and stood behind me, regarding me in the mirror. Darryl squinted, a visionary.

"Take off your clothes. We gotta start from scratch."

I barely paused, pulling off my T-shirt and stripping down to my boxers. I kept thinking of Kenny, the poor schlep who had rolled the bull tub over his toes. I wanted out of props and rigging.

Darryl looked at his clown buddies. "Happy or sad?" he asked.

"Sad," they said in unison.

"Hmm." Darryl looked again, nodded. "Sad." He cracked open his large makeup box and started removing tubes of makeup. "Close your eyes," he said.

I closed my eyes, feeling the warmth of the makeup lights on my eyelids. Then I felt cloth against my eyes.

"I'm just putting a cloth here so I don't get makeup in your eyes," he said.

"That's cool."

I felt the blindfold yanked tight around the back of my head. "Ow." I laughed nervously.

A large hand pushed me forward, planting my head on the plywood makeup bench. "What the fuck," I said, but someone already had my hands behind my back, and I heard the ripping sound of duct tape being pulled from the roll. My hands were bound, and another pair of hands was tearing my boxers down toward my ankles. More hands, hard on my hips, then a bobbing, rubbery cock against my bare skin.

I knew the only thing I had left was my legs. I pulled back my right leg and blindly mule-kicked as hard as I could. I was lucky. The sound was a fleshy cracking, and I followed through, feeling the knee snap backward. The grip on my hips disappeared. I followed with my feet again and again, landing about half my blows. My blindfold worked its way off one eye, and I could see the Fuck-You Clowns. The one they called Trout was finished; his friend was blacked out and broken up on the ground. I knew without the element of surprise that I wouldn't be so lucky with Darryl. As he advanced on me, I kicked a chair in his path and ran for the door, stumbling out into the darkness. My skateboard was lying there, and I pushed it forward with one foot, jumping on and kicking away, an absurd figure, naked, hands bound, speeding through the blighted parking lot. It didn't matter; Darryl wasn't following me. He'd had his recreation.

•

IT WASN'T UNTIL two weeks later that I had an opening on the dog. He was tied up around the corner from Hamburger Mary's, no one around. I fed him half a Snickers bar and shoved him in an empty paper-towel box I'd grabbed out of the trash.

I headed out into the Phoenix dusk. It was staggeringly hot, no wind, and as I kicked the skateboard, sweat drenched me and began to wet the cardboard box.

I'm not sure exactly what I had in mind as I skated away from the big top, but it was not ASPCA-friendly. I stopped a couple of times to check up on Pequin or Pepin. He just looked back at me, panting, appearing exhilarated by the ride. Finally I arrived in a real neighborhood, and as I went farther in, the houses got bigger, the lawns greener, and the streetlights more sporadic. These were the homes that housed people like my parents, with kids like I had once been: optimistic, innocent. A neighborhood full of potential victims.

I heard sounds and stopped. Through an opening in an estate wall, I could see a family at play in and around a lit pool. They were splashing and laughing, playing some kind of water-volleyball game. There were three kids, two boys and a girl, parents laughing and cheering them on.

I put the dog box in front of the front door and rang the doorbell a bunch of times. In case they couldn't hear out by the pool, I kicked the big Suburban parked in the driveway and got the alarm wailing.

I watched from the bushes as they discovered the dog. I watched the little girl, then the little boys, beg to keep the dog. The parents never had a chance. I could imagine their astonishment when their new dog pulled a perfect double backflip off the diving board.

TWENTY

THE BITCH ON THE COUCH

I WOKE WITH a start, sweating, as Sissy pushed against my shoulder.

"Hey, who's the bitch on the couch?"

"Her name's Xana."

"She your girlfriend?"

"No. She goes out with . . . somebody I know."

"Well, there's not enough room for both of you on the couch."

"Right." I was just starting to get my bearings. "Hey . . . your paintings are fantastic."

"That's what people tell me. I still don't have a gallery, though."

"I'll buy one—I mean, when I have some money."

"That's the other thing people tell me." She squinted at me. "Jesus."

"What?"

"Nothing."

"What?"

"You remind me of the last guy I let sleep over."

"Is that good?"

"Well, he stayed for two years and left with my car and my TV."

"Oh."

"I hated the TV, anyway."

"How about the car?"

"No, I liked the car."

"Sorry."

"You have nothing to apologize for, unless you plan on taking something else."

"No . . . I'm just . . . really glad I had somebody I

could ask for help. You're kind of the only person I know out here who doesn't want to kill me or think I'm already dead."

Sissy gestured into the living room. "What about her?"

"I'm not too sure about her. But she's not in any position to help me."

"So . . ." She looked at me flatly. I was in her bed.

"Oh. Sorry. If you have a blanket or something, I can crash on the floor."

She nodded. "I'm gonna take a shower. There's a sleeping bag in the closet."

I closed my eyes, and when I opened them again, Sissy stood before me wrapped in a towel.

"Why do you think I like you?" she asked, as if we had been in the middle of a conversation.

"I have absolutely no idea."

"I don't, either," she said.

She knelt on the bed next to me and laid her hand flat on my chest. "Is this a terrible idea?" she asked.

"Probably."

"Yeah. You're fucked up."

"Yeah."

"I always go for the fucked-up ones."

COPPING FREE

I nodded. She came down on top of me and kissed my mouth.

Her mouth tasted of baking-soda toothpaste and oranges, sharp and surprising, unlike any mouth that had ever been against mine. I was immediately awake, the wet terry cloth giving way to her cool blue-white skin. I kissed her hands and the wrecked veins on her arms. We collapsed into each other. Something inevitable was taking place, something at the edge of control.

TWENTY-ONE

An Olive Branch up Your Ass

IT WAS EARLY, just before daylight. The mockingbird was going off again, mournful and alone and absurd, calling into the darkness, trying to attract a mate. I slid out of bed. Sissy lay on her back with her hair tangled up, her mouth in a small "O," one freckled breast and one pale nipple showing. In repose she was perfect. She had disappeared into the burning land of damage and risen again, whole and somehow fortified, like porcelain from the kiln. I was still somewhere deep in the smoldering wreckage. The only thing I could do was drag her back in; there was no potential upside to time spent with me. But here I was insinuating myself into her carefully crafted existence, her quiet world of Mocus, painting, busing. I knew the best possible option was for me to grab Xana and go, find a shitty motel to hunker down in, and figure out a way to die as painlessly as possible. But I figured the least I could do was bring Sissy coffee and some breakfast, take Mocus for a walk, not just abandon her after taking advantage of her kindness and her pale, luminous body.

Xana was sleeping on the couch in the exact position I had left her in; her ability to sleep through any horror would probably be the thing that saved her. I found Mocus's leash and tried to put it on as he danced around the kitchen in anticipation of his walk.

I found a coffee place on Abbott Kinney Boulevard and got myself a cappuccino. I sat outside with Mocus and read through two newspapers as I watched the sky grow light.

I was savoring my last moment of quiet. The coffee almost mocked me with its simple domesticity, its promise of a day so unadorned that it would require caffeine to stay awake through it. On the street, a father and son rode by on skateboards, the father shouting, "Dig in! Dig in!" I bought coffee and pastries for Sissy and Xana and walked back toward the house. When I got to the door, it felt wrong, like the seconds before an earthquake. I stepped into the house, with Mocus still on his leash, and before I could see what was happening, the dog lunged toward the couch where Shane sat, filthy and shaken.

"Mocus!" Sissy said.

I pulled on the leash and stopped the big rottweiler just short of Shane.

"Let him go, Bailey, I'm dead meat anyway," Shane said.

I looked Shane over. He was taut and pathetic, quivering, traumatized. I handed the leash to Sissy.

"Yeah, you're dead. But I'm not gonna give the dog the pleasure," I said.

"No, you don't understand, dude. I'm here to give you, like, an olive branch."

"An olive branch from the guy who tried to off me?"

"Totally."

"How 'bout if I shove an olive branch up your ass?"

"Please, Bailey . . . I'm scared, man. I'm fuckin' scared."

I moved toward him with a cocked fist. Sissy stepped into the space between us, slackening the cord of pure malice. Mocus growled from somewhere deep in his rottweilerness.

"I don't know what's going on with you people, but anything bad happens outside this house." Sissy snapped the leash, and the growl stopped utterly.

"Wait," I said. I nodded to Xana. "See if he's carrying that stupid gun."

Xana knew just where the gun lived. She pulled up Shane's left pant leg. Sure enough, he had the chrome nine holstered there, looking overly polished and fetishized. It was so heavy I was surprised he could even walk.

"Hand it to me," I said to Xana, unsure whether she would unload the clip on me. She looked up at Shane, who gave his head a resigned, vapid nod. Xana unbuttoned the smoothly burnished leather holster—a crazy fetish object all its own—and unsheathed the gun in a worshipful, overtly sexual gesture of submission. She handed me the piece with an abstracted smile and backed away from Shane.

I hefted the gun in my hand and looked at Shane. I aimed from the hip as if to shoot him, almost unconsciously, but I realized in time that I had flicked off the safety and that my trigger finger was tapping nervously on the side of the stock.

"Bailey, what the fuck are you doing? I can get us money, Bailey! I can get us out of this with the Freaks . . . Please, man!" It was nice to hear Shane beg.

Sissy yelled, "Don't you fucking dare shoot this guy in my house! I'm still on probation, you stupid shit!"

"He tried to kill me," I said.

"I watched what they did to Timbo and Raol," Shane said. "They were gonna do me, but I got away. I slugged the creepy dude that smells like gasoline and carries around the chick that looks like a bowling pin. No—like a fuckin' harp seal."

He was planning to go on, but I kicked him hard across the legs and shut him up. I thought of Eelie Willow, the Limbless Lady. My former lover. My confidante. And I realized none of this was about forty-five thousand dollars. This was about another, much more grave betrayal. This was the age-old story of a woman scorned. And she was fully in the process of unleashing her fury. On me. The other guys were a necessary annoyance, more of a warm-up act. Eelie was gunning for me. She wouldn't be happy with the money alone; she wouldn't even pause when she got her flippers on the cash. She was marching steadily toward a showdown with Bailey Quinn, criminal, college dropout, drug addict, loser, dead man. She was only borrowing the legs and sociopathy of her husband and the other Freaks, I was sure of that now. This was entirely personal. I kicked Shane again, because it felt good and he didn't seem to care.

"Just give me my money and I'll blow outta here and you can fuck off into thin air," I said.

"It's gone."

"What . . . what's gone?"

"The money. It's gone."

I looked down at the vinyl pattern on Sissy's floor. It was a geometrical swirl, and it seemed to be calling me, hypnotizing. I took two steps toward Shane and, without breaking stride, punched him as hard as I could in the face. I felt my middle finger break and some of Shane's teeth push through his lower lip. We both grabbed our wounded parts, and I immediately regretted not hitting him with the butt of his own stupid gun. That was exactly what this type of gun was made for, pistol-whipping partners in crime who had betrayed you. Jumping into character, Shane started whining.

"Just fucking shoot me, Bailey! We're dead anyway, just shoot my ass!"

"Shut up, Shane," Xana said.

"Nobody is shooting anybody in my house," Sissy said.

In answer to Sissy's mandate, I held up the gun and dropped the clip in my hand and pocketed it. My broken finger throbbed a crazed salsa beat. I was feeling desperate and floaty, the coffee, the lack of sleep, the certainty of approaching death all swirling together into a sour, intoxicating cocktail.

"Whatta you mean, the money's gone?" I asked.

"Like gone. Like no longer in my possession."

"And where has it gone, Shane?" Now I was sounding like a detective on an A&E reality-show reenactment. I felt the need to get high, to run through the moonlight tripping out of my head. I missed college.

"I made a deal with some guys." Suddenly Shane sounded upbeat, smiling crazily through his bloody mouth.

"For what? Magic beans?"

"Speed gear."

I imagined my nemesis in an aerodynamic bodysuit, luging to Olympic gold. "What're you talking about?"

"Investing it. Buying equipment to make a crystal superlab."

"No. Please tell me you didn't—"

"It's pure profit, Bailey. We'll turn it into half a million in a couple of months. It was Xana's idea."

"I know some guys who deal in all that stuff," said Xana. She smiled hopefully, willing me not to shoot her. "Shane knows a place where we can cook it. Some trailer up by Salmon."

"Oh, Christ. Where? When?"

"Bailey . . ." Xana winced.

"Tell me. Right fucking now."

I remembered that Shane had briefly cooked crystal meth in an old miner's cabin out in Bumfuck, Idaho. According to him, he'd netted big Benjamins for a few weeks' work.

"Please don't tell me you gave my money to a bunch of tweakers," I said. I pulled the ammo clip back out of my pocket for emphasis.

"I did, Bailey, but it's an awesome deal! You're gonna be into it, I guarantee you! It's a straight shot down the rapids, dude! You are gonna shit yourself! I gave them the forty K, right?"

"There was forty-five."

"Whatever. Incidentals and shit. And in return, they give us our own lab and a couple of wetbacks to do the dangerous work. And dude, we make *fifty* percent of our gross! You know what kinda crazy money that is? What kinda sick green we could pull in over a couple of months?"

"Who's 'they'? A bunch of underweight white supremacists?"

"No, dude! The Skullfuckers!"

I blanched, all semblance of a cool-guy act giving way to bowel-loosening panic. The Skullfuckers. Even the cops left these guys alone. The Hells Angels were a bunch of whiny nine-year-old bitches next to the Skullfuckers. I had heard stories—hell, everyone had heard stories about the Skullfuckers. Their initiation involved rape, sodomy, and murder, and from there they worked their way up. They had been linked to a network of ice labs from San Diego to Maine. They were rich, stoned, and still pissed off. They ate co-eds like me for a light palate-cleanser, like a raspberry sorbet.

"Where is it?"

"Um, I don't have it yet. We're supposed to pick it up tonight."

"Who's we?"

"We. Us. You and me, bro. Together again! I got your back!"

TWENTY-TWO

A Confusion of Ecstasy

HERE'S THE DEAL: I have a pretty good criminal mind. I may even be a sociopath. Well, maybe not a sociopath, but I have a level of amorality that allows me to get the job done. Then, sadly, there's the human factor, the strand of DNA that helps me choose my associates, my victims, and my marks. In this regard, I can't claim to be a Capone. Take my long con on Eelie Willow as an example. I selected her out of all the other potential marks among the Freaks, and I thought I had chosen wisely. She was vulnerable both emotionally and physically; she liked me; we had an excellent rapport from the beginning. How did it come to be such an unmitigated disaster? I could be a good sociopath and blame others, but I think it comes right down to the man in the mirror. I fell in love with the Limbless Lady.

AFTER I HANDED in my drawings of Eelie's Trailer Self-Reliance Unit (that's what I titled the sketches) I felt like a minor celebrity. Trying to appear unemotional, Eelie praised them succinctly. Even Arnold was uncharacteristically generous in his praise.

"Looks like you gone to drawin' school," he said.

I nodded. "Sort of."

"You think you can make her something that looks like these drawings? Something that works?"

I swallowed hard. I knew if he paid me and I failed, things could quickly get gnarly and the goodwill would evaporate like acetone, fast and with a foul odor.

"Yeah, I think I could. Might take a little while, though."

"That mean you're gonna be sniffin' around my trailer all hours?"

"No, only when the show is down and I have free time."

He nodded and rubbed his filthy, pockmarked face. "I'd like her to feel empowered," he said stupidly.

I guffawed aloud, then turned it into a cough. Clearly Arnold had spent a few afternoons cracking open Budweisers in front of *Dr. Phil*.

I cleared my throat and said professionally, "Well, Arnold, I think this device could go a long way toward helping her to achieve some independence."

"Yeah, but I don't want her thinkin' she's fine without me," he said, apparently not feeling any discomfort from the contradiction.

"Right. Well, I'm sure she'd never think that."

"No way, Jose!" He seemed to be done with me.

"So, should I start to work on the trailer?"

Arnold sucked air through his gapped teeth. "Yeah, what the hell. It's her money, anyway."

"Cool."

COPPING FREE

"Yeah. 'Cool,'" Arnold mocked. He clearly hated me, and seemed ready to smite me. But he didn't have a club or a broadsword, so he shook his head and disappeared inside the trailer.

I kicked away on my skateboard, my head swirling with possibilities. But something else was at the forefront, something that was keeping me from planning my perfect crime. It was Eelie. I was most excited about getting to spend time with her. I don't know a lot about being a con man, but I'm reasonably certain your heart is not supposed to skip a beat at the thought of spending time with your mark.

When I came around one of the honeywagons, I almost collided with Eelie.

"Hey, Speedy, what's up?"

I knelt to talk to her, even though I wanted nothing more than to pick her up and hold her in my arms. "I just showed your husband the plans."

"Did you two have fun?"

"We had a great time."

"Does that mean he didn't actually hit you?"

"Not only that, he gave me the go-ahead."

Her grimace-smile gave way to a flash of delight, if

only for a second. "Guess that means you'll be around some."

"I guess so. If that works for you."

"I'm pretty sure I'll adjust." She looked up right into my eyes. "He's going to town to buy supplies tomorrow at three. I better go."

I watched her flipper away on her skateboard rig.

It wasn't like I knew I was doing two things that didn't jive. I didn't know that I was so far into my mark, that I was heading down a path that would eventually lead me into territories for which I had no road map.

AT ABOUT THREE the next day, I watched, hunkered beside one of the trailers, as Arnold left his trailer with Baby and Bezio. I followed them to the parking lot and watched until they had completely disappeared, the pickup truck vanishing into the shimmering heat of Amarillo.

I knocked on the door of the trailer.

"It's open," Eelie said.

I walked inside. There was a scent in the air, not roses or gardenia but something tropical, exotic, almost obscenely fecund and ripe. A few candles were burning, making the trailer look like a gypsy's cart.

"Come here."

I heard her, though I couldn't yet see her. When I stepped farther into the trailer, there she lay, naked, obscured by only a very sheer top sheet, her face framed by her thick black hair, her magnificent breasts; her flippers were shrouded, a beguiling mystery beneath the covers.

"Take off your clothes," she commanded simply. I complied like a zombie, dropping trou and everything else in a matter of seconds.

"Lie down on your back."

I lay down next to her. Her crazy tropical scent was creating a heightened sexual state in which all I could do was tremble and emit an almost inaudible whimper. I reached toward her shoulder, or the place where her flipper met her chest.

"Just lie back and close your eyes, sweet Bailey," she whispered.

I closed my eyes. If I had been in a heightened sexual state, I was now reaching a sexual plateau, albeit a dangerous one. She worked her way on top of me, shoving my hands away when I tried to help her. Then she kissed me in a way that was both sacred and prurient, wet, urgent. What followed can only be described as a confusion of ecstasy.

As she made her way over my body, I kept my eyes closed, per her orders. I am to this day unsure which part was touching, sucking, or massaging. I know for certain that I made sounds not unlike my old cat, Tinkerbell, before we put her to sleep. This went on for I have no idea how long. Things got quiet for a second, and when my eyes flickered open, Eelie was on top of me.

"Now you can help," she said.

I took her by the waist and lowered her onto me. Now I was completely in control. Eelie only looked back at me with a serene, limpid gaze.

You know the way guys are always talking about a spinner? The girl who's tiny and athletic and all but pirouettes around your cock? Well, Eelie was an *actual* spinner. I moved her up and down, around and around, up into the air over my head. . . . I felt like young Nureyev partnering some prima ballerina.

IT ONLY GOT better. The closer we got to being caught by Arnold, the more exciting it became. But Arnold was not even suspicious, because work on the Trailer Self-

Reliance Unit was progressing smoothly. I felt I could balance my deceit of Eelie by delivering her real freedom, from her handicap, from her hideous husband, from the need to invite in predators like me.

After our bouts of Olympian lovemaking, Eelie was as open as a 7-Eleven. She would talk in long, breathy stream-of-consciousness sentences about her difficult childhood, about performing in the sideshow, and about her lousy marriage to Arnold. It was in these moments that I learned all the information necessary to pull off the payroll heist. She confirmed what I had suspected, that the Freaks worked entirely in cash and did not employ an outside payroll company; that, for tax-evasion purposes, the accounting was fudged. I also learned about the cash flow, when the cash sat in one place before it was dispersed into pay envelopes. I was given, by my limited but enthusiastic lover, everything I needed to pull off the job.

When I jumped off the circus—for some reason, they called it jumping off instead of quitting—I had completed the Trailer Self-Reliance Unit for Eelie. I unveiled it to her first, a series of simple lever and pulley mechanisms that would change her life. She was grateful, overjoyed, girlish. I could barely meet her gaze, because as much as I was giving her, I would also be taking away.

TWENTY-THREE

KILL TO RIDE, RIDE TO KILL

I HONESTLY CAN'T say why I went to the desert with Shane. I thought maybe there was a chance I could ask for my piece of the money back, that I could explain I no longer believed in copping free, that I didn't want to be a part of a meth lab, didn't want to make tweakers out of fourteen-year-olds. That I wanted Raol and Timbo to be alive again.

The highway through the so-called Inland Empire was a crowded, multilaned expressway lined with a series of blighted fast-food ghettos, car dealerships, train yards, and Indian casinos. This was not the land I remembered from my magical childhood trip to Disneyland. The color in the landscape seemed to have been painstakingly removed pixel by pixel, until what remained was a washed-out sunscape punctuated by the bright oranges and yellows of the McDonald's and Burger King signs.

I had pulled the VW bus out of retirement, possibly a foolish move, but at least a foolish move on top of already foolish moves. It was the only way we could all travel together. Sissy had decided to join us, against my wishes, on the condition that she would stay in the car while the deal went down. Xana had fallen asleep while Shane nursed his broken nose and drank shots from a bottle of peppermint schnapps he had insisted on buying at a rest stop. Mocus lay curled next to Xana, while Sissy sat next to me up front. As much as I had protested, I was glad Sissy was here. Her mere presence soothed me, unlike that of Shane, which felt like a bag of two-week-old garbage, foul and unwanted.

All in all, we were a pathetic little squad next to the

Skullfuckers, who had a reputation for beheading their enemies and impaling the severed heads to display as a warning to others. The Skullfuckers, whose emblem bore the likeness of a switchblade through the eye socket of a maggoty skull—whose motto, "Kill to Ride, Ride to Kill," was striking in its declarative simplicity— were the men against whom I was going into battle. My hope was that under the neo-pirate swagger, behind the swastika tattoos and smelly beards, there would be a human being among the lot of them who would understand a mistake had been made, and, criminal to criminal, they could help straighten it out. They would give me a portion of my well-earned money; Shane would take less in the way of meth-lab setup; and I would quietly disappear.

On the other hand, they could stick a gun in my mouth and pull the trigger; the less desirable outcome.

We were starting to enter the Coachella Valley, an unimpressive gouge in the landscape that looked more like a wound than a geographical feature. I was starting to sweat, regretting the decision to make this trip at all, feeling swept into a tide of fate more than anything approaching a rationale. Mocus stood up and gingerly made his way between the seats, presenting his massive head for some rubbing. I scratched and rubbed between his ears and eyes, and he opened his mouth into what looked startlingly like a smile. I looked over at Sissy, who was also checking Mocus out. Our eyes met. She reached out to pet Mocus, and her hand grazed mine. I put my hand over hers, drinking in her steady, purposeful calm. She smiled and turned her hand over, so that we were holding hands on the vast plateau of Mocus's head.

I had actually met someone I could imagine spending time with, real time, like the-rest-of-my-life kind of time. Strangely, the two women I had most recently slept with were in the car with me. But I wished I could erase everything that had happened with Xana. It was the mistake of a horny, traumatized youth. If I had the chance, I would spend every moment of the rest of my life trying to be a worthwhile person for Sissy.

"My face feels like shit," Shane moaned from the back.

"Shut up," I said. "And stop drinking."

"I need to drink because my face feels like shit."

"Look, we're almost there. You're gonna shut the fuck up and let me do the talking. Every time you open your mouth, something bad happens."

"Why don't you stop harshing on me, Bailey? You think I'm happy about the way things turned out? They were my friends, too."

"Yeah, and you got them killed. Just like you tried to kill me. So shut the *fuck* up and stop hitting the schnapps."

"I'm just trying to stay mellow."

"I swear to God, Shane, I'm gonna pull over and shoot you if you don't shut up."

I saw our exit coming up, and my stomach trap-doored on me. I realized I hadn't taken a decent breath for hours, so I tried to suck in some air and focus on my immediate task: Get in, recover some cash, get out alive. Leave Shane and Xana and the Skullfuckers in my rearview.

I followed the directions off the freeway through a series of subdivisions with optimistic names like Golden Hills and Chardonnay Gardens, which stubbornly refused to acknowledge the truth—that they were tiny outposts in the void, separated from the endless desert by a few sad structures and a sprinkler system.

We were getting closer. I entered the subdivision grandly named Phoenix Estates, with a sign bearing a glossy Italianate sign painter's rendering of the mythical bird. The name was all the more incongruous for the place it was depicting. This was a subdivision that, for whatever reason—bankruptcy, downturn in the economy, toxic spillage—had never been occupied. The houses were almost all completed but had obviously sat abandoned for some time. A few of them were huge, ten thousand square feet, all with that vaguely Tuscan look so popular in the nineties. Although there were NO TRESPASSING signs everywhere, the houses had been roundly vandalized: broken windows, graffiti, bullet holes.

We wound deeper and deeper into the wrecked subdivision. Suddenly everyone was acting out the agita of the moment: Shane was conspicuously silent, Xana wide awake, Mocus standing, Sissy bouncing one knee up and down. I pulled off onto a side street.

"I'm gonna park up here," I said. "We'll walk the rest of the way." I figured we were at least a quarter mile away from the address. I looked at Sissy. "You're staying here with Mocus. If anything weird happens, just drive."

"Why would anything weird happen?" Shane wouldn't keep his mouth shut. "We're getting our shit and leaving."

"That's right, Shane. And you're keeping your fuck-ing mouth shut the whole time."

"Whatever, bossman."

I pulled the bus over and got out, followed by Xana and Shane. My legs were like quivering lead, and my bowels were jumpy and disgruntled. This was what they referred to in military circles as "go time."

I looked at Sissy, and something passed between us, an understanding, or possibly something deeper, an im-plicit vow: If I emerged from this thing alive and whole, I would be there for her the way she had been there for me, simply and totally and without affect.

The cul-de-sac bowled out in the center, giving me the feeling that our group were like tiny animals or fish in a cramped aquarium. We stood at the front door, and I could smell the acrid aroma of meth cooking. This was officially a bad idea. I realized that none of us was reaching for the door. Xana and Shane were waiting for me. I pressed the doorbell and heard nothing. Then pressed it again, then raised my hand to knock as the door opened. I must have blinked ten times before any of us said or did anything, because I honestly wasn't sure if the guy standing before me was real or I had conjured him from the depths of my sad and dented psyche. He

COPPING FREE

was at least six-five, Ramones–thin, with glassed-out, demonic eyes and filthy black hair down to his ass. Probably at least half American Indian. His eyes darted back and forth like one of those retro cat clocks, and his jaw muscles seemed to gnash and pop rhythmically with each eye dart. His body was covered with a combination of scabs, jailhouse tats, and legit ink whose cumulative effect was that of a man who'd rolled in a pile of wet comic books.

"Ah, yes. Greetings, little ones. Greetings. Ha!"

So on top of everything else, he was going to talk like a Yu-Gi-Oh! character.

I couldn't look in those crazed tweaker eyes, so my eyes darted down, and what I saw sucked the breath out of me like a line drive to the solar plexus: a tattoo around his neck, identical in every way to Bezio's, down to the last piece of rotted flesh, down to the last over-grown fingernail. Bezio was a Skullfucker. It was a setup.

I turned to run, but walking toward us down the cul-de-sac was as terrifying an amalgam as I have ever witnessed: the Freaks.

TWENTY-FOUR

KILL HIM, DARLING

BEZIO, BABY, ARNOLD, and in his arms, Eelie. Nobody in the world is more recognizable than Eelie, but I did a double take and had to reorganize my perception of her. I realized it was her face that was throwing me off. She had lost something. Her social face, the ironic one, I had never seen her in public without it. But here she was, serious, steely, no grimace, irony-free. Our dalliance had cost her her worldview. I was so fixated on her, I had hardly noticed that Baby was holding an angry-looking sawed-off shotgun, and Arnold, repugnant even in his weapon choice, an old Luger, which seemed to extend directly from Eelie's rib cage.

"Shane, you are such a loser," I said. "Do you really think they're gonna let you walk away from this?"

"Dude, I didn't reach out to these guys. You kidding?"

We both turned and looked at Xana. She shrugged coyly. "They were either gonna kill me or pay me five large. Sorry."

When Xana was hiding under the mattress doing her best imitation of a terrified waif, she was working me, like she had worked everybody she'd ever met. She even sold out the sellout, Shane.

Shane stood there, mouth agape, staring at Xana, apparently unable to comprehend that his little flower would be capable of such deceit.

"Don't look so shocked, Shane," I said. "She threw me a bang along the way, too."

"You fucking bitch," he said.

"Step inside, children," said Yu-Gi-Oh! Indian Guy. "You know how the neighbors gossip."

We backed inside the house, littered with empty boxes of cold medicine, a key ingredient in the production of ice. It was a classic tweaker setup: junk-food wrappers, strange, obsessive clusters of objects overly and crazily arranged next to filth and squalor. A series of shoes, organized by size, four feet from a mess of week-old vomit. A giant pyramid of soda cans. Tweakers were forever getting inspired to clean and arrange things as the sun was coming up after they had been ice-bingeing for days on end. I didn't get a good feeling about talking reasonably with these folks. But right now they were not my immediate worry. Eelie was fixed on me, utterly beamed in and staring, tuning out everyone and everything else around her.

"Bring me close to him, honey," Eelie murmured to Arnold.

"That's sweet, isn't it, boys?" said Arnold. "She wants to be close to her lover-boy."

I was beginning to wonder if Arnold had been dipping into the crystal, because his mouth and jaw were shaking, and his eyes were glazed and bugging. But then I realized he was high, not on speed but on his all-consuming rage, and at the nearness to his prey. He was going to kill me and love it. I had a flash of what had happened to Timbo and Raol, the pornographic quality of their murders, the violation, the entry, the burn.

Something clicked in, a small cry for survival, a desire to live, maybe for myself, maybe simply so Sissy wouldn't have to endure yet another horrible disappointment, another loser pinballing through her life. I looked around for more Skullfuckers, and all I could see were a couple of Mexicans humping around the incredibly toxic, flammable chemicals.

Arnold was grinning now, wild-eyed, bringing Eelie closer to me. She was heavy-lidded, on the verge of some kind of euphoria, like a tent-show revivalist getting ready for the snake handling.

"Closer, honey. I want to get really close."

"Yeah, get close to your lover-boy."

"Closer, baby."

Arnold had come as close as he possibly could, and now began to proffer Eelie forward, like he was offering her up for some ritual or baptism. I felt the cool, smooth skin of her cheek against mine, her hair cascading down onto my neck, and for a second I was transported to our rapturous lovemaking sessions, when she would writhe over my body, pushing, probing, dragging her hair across my belly and over my hard cock. I wanted to tell her I was sorry, really sorry, that I had taken some of what little she had to begin with.

I had closed my eyes, and when I opened them, she was looking into my eyes, not more than an inch away.

"Push me in, Arnold," she whispered.

Arnold moved her closer, open and plaintive, like an old, distorted painting of the baby Jesus.

She whispered so softly that even up against her, I had to strain slightly to hear her.

"You broke my heart," she said.

I felt her lips brush mine, then a searing, venomous pain ripping through my face.

"Fuck yeah!" Baby said, backing away with a balletic, mincing step.

Eelie still looked right into my eyes, blood dripping down her lips and chin. She spat out a good-sized piece of flesh. Arnold blinked manically, as if he couldn't believe his eyes. I staggered back a step, raising my hand to my cheek. A seeping warmth flowed down my face, into my mouth, down my neck, and into my shirt.

I was either going to black out or make a move. Or some combination of the two. I crouched and put my hands to my face. The throb was intense, and I knew I was losing blood, maybe not a fatal amount, but some had already made its way all the way into my shoes.

Xana leaned over next to me. "Bailey, you okay?"

"Nahh . . ." I said vaguely.

"What the fuck are you doing, Xana?" It was Shane, ever the inopportune speaker. "You rushing to the side of your little fuck-buddy? That what you're doing, you fucking piece of shit?"

I staggered down to one knee, which drew the attention momentarily from Shane, giving him time to pull a piece from somewhere between his shoulder blades. Where did this guy get all the weapons? He fired two shots into Xana and one into Bezio before Baby fired, launching Shane off his feet with the impact. He landed a good four feet back on his ass, the gun clattering and sliding across the vast living room. There was the briefest lull as Shane sat there, blood spattering out his mouth as he drew his last labored breaths.

I knew the whole thing was in the process of shitting the bed. The Mexicans were scrambling in the deep background. The big tattooed Indian was still gawking at Xana, who was alive enough to be doing a pretty spectacular death dance. Bezio was winged and struggling, and no one even seemed to care that I was gushing blood from the face.

"Kill him, darling," said Eelie.

Arnold was rearranging Eelie so he could get off a shot at me, and Baby was racking the shotgun, probably also looking to add some lead to my body. The Indian pulled a big bowie knife, lifted Xana by the hair, and slashed her throat with a sudden and expert violence, causing her to immediately quiet, then bleed out in one massive, gurgling rush.

"Feels fuckin' good!" he said, wiping the knife blade on his leg.

I was still partly doubled over but watching everything carefully. Baby, Arnold, Eelie, and the Indian were momentarily focused on Xana's death mask, but I was the last and most alive piece of business remaining. I inched the .22 out of my belt and fired two shots straight into Baby's huge belly. Arnold was leveling a big pistol at me, and the Indian was moving in with the bowie knife. I couldn't make a choice. I hesitated, and in my hesitation, I was fucked.

I decided to turn and take Arnold's bullet straight on. But something crossed my vision—a perfectly horizontal rottweiler about three feet in the air.

Mocus hit Arnold about midchest. To his credit, Arnold chose to hang on to his mobility-challenged spouse, forsaking all others, including himself. Mocus tore into the back of Arnold's neck as he valiantly protected Eelie. Sissy swooped in behind Mocus and swung a tire iron right into the sweet spot of Baby's head just as he was about to plug me. Baby fell like a bag of wet concrete. I was able to get a shot into the Indian tweaker before the .22 jammed. He fell facedown and slid his hand across the big bowie blade after it stuck in the floor. The last thing he saw were three of his fingers rolling off his hand and settling next to his cheek.

"Run, Bailey . . . through the back . . . there's a bunch more bikers pulling up outside."

Sissy was right. I could hear the aggressive idling of Harleys in the quiet cul-de-sac. I pushed my hand into my throbbing cheek, grateful to have someone to follow. I picked Arnold's gun up as Sissy pulled Mocus off his back. My last image of that tableau of gore was Eelie trying to wiggle her way out from under her bloodied husband as we ran for the back door.

We bolted through the kitchen. The Mexican lab guys were running around freaking out, trying to get out the door. The lab was pretty extensive, what they called a superlab on the local news whenever they busted one. The smell was overwhelmingly sickening, and there was a staggering amount of flammable material in one place. I was so weak and so focused on getting out of there that I only took it all in peripherally.

The front door opened with a hollow shattering sound. Sounds of heavy motorcycle boots thundered toward us, and I caught sight of a stampede of bikers—the hard-core contingent of Skullfuckers—looking like ravaged Norse gods unleashed from some hellish Valhalla.

Sissy paused in the kitchen as if we weren't about to die. She began tipping the nasty, blackened cook pots, which caused the mixtures to smoke and become even more unstable.

"Shoot, Bailey!" she shouted. I had no idea—Did she want me to open fire on the Skullfuckers? From the sound of it, there were half a dozen of them at least.

"The speed! Shoot the speed!"

We moved to the back door of the huge house, and I leveled the .22 at the stove, brimming with chemicals, surrounded by even more chemicals. The Skullfuckers had just rounded the corner into the kitchen and hesitated at the sight of the gun. One of the huge trolls reached into his vest, and I saw the butt of a pistol. I closed my eyes, praying the cheap gun wasn't still jammed, and fired in rapid succession, planning to empty the clip. But on the second shot, Sissy pulled me back from the glass door. We were blown back from the house, Mocus thrown cleanly across both of us. Glass, wood, and stucco rained down from the wrecked house. The entire second floor was buckling into the kitchen, which was burning white hot and continuing to send off new explosions. I held tightly to Sissy's hand and lifted her from the ground. Remarkably, we were all on our feet, even the big rottweiler, who had taken the brunt of the blast. When we reached the top of the cul-de-sac, the entire house was ablaze, but other than the flames, which did a primitive and unstoppable dance, there was no movement below.

TWENTY-FIVE

A SEXY SCAR

THERE ARE WILD parrots here. No kidding. They come up from Mexico or someplace, when the weather warms up in the spring. They scream like crazed lovers, fighting over the seeds that grow on the palm trees in our yard. They make me laugh, because to them, everything is equally, frantically important. They careen drunkenly in and out of the trees, and their arrival is a giddy reminder that spring is here, even in L.A., where it's never fully winter. I get out the old surfboard I bought at a yard sale—an eight-foot funshape—and wax it and repair the dings and wait for the swell to fill in so I can go in the ocean and make an idiot out of myself.

Sissy has her first show at a gallery in Venice, and she's already sold three pieces, one to a guy who played the android sidekick on one of those *Star Trek* spin-offs. Sissy got me a gig at Ivy at the Shore. I started as a dishwasher, which totally blew, but then I got promoted to garde-manger, which is fancy restaurantese for "salad guy." Dudley Do-Right still works there—his name is Phillip and he's actually an okay guy. I'm taking a pretty full load of classes at Santa Monica College, but I think I may try to go after the cooking thing. Chefs rule.

I think a lot about Eelie, struggling to get out from under Arnold, about what she must have felt like in that burning house, about the things that led to that moment, the weird suburban slum in the desert, about how she was just this person who wanted love, and how the love blossomed like a crazy weed into her desire for revenge. I think about that piece of my cheek left behind, sizzling and popping in the unforgiving heat (Sissy says my scar is sexy). I think about my mother and her own wrecked love, her head on that scalloped bath pillow in her final angle of repose.

I think about whether any of them survived. From what I could tell in the papers, nobody did, and no one seemed to have a clue as to what happened in the speed lab, or as they called it in the newspaper, the superlab. I think about if one of those bikers got out, or Arnold, and if they would ever try to finish what they had started. If they do, I feel weirdly unafraid, like I paid for what happened already, and I feel like no matter what, no one can touch us. We're here, right here on Brooks Avenue in Venice, California. So bring it if you want to, motherfuckers. We'll be here.

Me, Sissy, Mocus: not the family I ever imagined, but maybe the one I was heading for all along.

PHOTO: HELEN HUNT

MATTHEW CARNAHAN has had seventy-seven jobs, from deckhand to circus worker. He studied at New York University and the Neighborhood Playhouse School of the Theatre. After working as a playwright and director in New York, Carnahan received the Chesterfield Writer's Film Project fellowship from Steven Spielberg. His feature directorial debut, *Black Circle Boys,* premiered at the Sundance Film Festival, as did his film *Mailman.* He also directed *Rudyland,* the award-winning documentary about former New York City mayor Rudolph Giuliani. Carnahan is currently working on a new novel. He lives in Southern California and New York City with his girlfriend, Helen; son, Emmett; and daughter, Mákena lei. Visit his web site at www.MatthewCarnahan.com.